Transparency

Transparency

Stories

FRANCES HWANG

BACK BAY BOOKS
Little, Brown and Company
NEW YORK   BOSTON   LONDON

Back Bay Books / Little, Brown and Company
Hachette Book Group USA
237 Park Avenue, New York, NY 10169
Visit our Web site at www.HachetteBookGroupUSA.com

First Edition: April 2007

The characters and events in this book are fictitious. Any similarity to real persons, living or dead, is coincidental and not intended by the author.

Grateful acknowledgment is made to the publishers of earlier versions of these stories: *Tin House* and *Best of Tin House* ("The Old Gentleman"), *Shankpainter* ("Remedies"), *AGNI Online* ("Giving a Clock"), *The Madison Review* ("Blue Hour"), *Best New American Voices 2003* ("Transparency"), *Subtropics* ("Intruders"), and *Glimmer Train* and *Best New American Voices 2005* ("Garden City").

In "The Old Gentleman," the quotations on pages 3 and 4 by Cao Xueqin appear in his novel *The Story of the Stone,* translated by David Hawkes (Penguin Books, 1973). The line of verse quoted on page 9 by Meng Chiao is from "Failing the Examination," translated by Stephen Owen and published in *Sunflower Splendor,* which was coedited by Wu-chi Liu and Irving Yucheng Lo (Indiana University Press, 1975). On page 31, Lily's recollections of her husband's calligraphy being burned by the state were inspired by a true story published in *Chinese Lives* by Zhang Xinxin and Sang Ye (Pantheon Books, 1987). In "Sonata for the Left Hand," the verse recited on page 133 is from Horace's "Diffugere nives," Ode 4.7, translated by A. E. Housman and published in his collection *More Poems* (Alfred A. Knopf, 1936).

Library of Congress Cataloging-in-Publication Data

Hwang, Frances.
   Transparency: stories / Frances Hwang. — 1st ed.
     p.   cm.
   ISBN: 978-0-316-16693-5
   1. Immigrants — Fiction. I. Title.
   PS3608.W37T73 2007
   813'.6 — dc22   2006028395

          10   9   8   7   6   5   4   3   2   1

                          Q-MART

Printed in the United States of America

Book design by Brooke Koven

For my parents,
Nancy and Jau-Fu Hwang

CONTENTS

Transparency

THE OLD GENTLEMAN

As a young girl, Agnes was often embarrassed by her father. Her family lived on the compound of a girls' high school in Taipei where her father worked as principal. On Monday mornings, after the flag had been raised and the national anthem sung, he liked to give speeches to the students assembled in the main courtyard. To get their attention, he stood with silent, aggrieved humility, his arms dangling at his sides, his limp suit already wrinkled from the humid weather, the front pockets stuffed with his reading glasses, a spiral notebook, a pack of cigarettes, and a well-used handkerchief. When he opened his mouth, he did not immediately speak, desiring that slight pause, that moment of breath in which everyone's attention was fixed on him alone. He quoted regularly from Mengzi, but his favorite writer was Cao Xueqin. " 'Girls are made of water and boys are made of mud,' " he declared. Or " 'The pure essence of humanity is concentrated in the female of the species. Males are its mere dregs and off-scourings.' " He clasped his hands behind his back, his eyes widening as he spoke. "Each of you is capable, but you must cultivate within yourself a sense of honesty and shame." He reminded the girls to rinse their mouths out with tea when they said a dirty word. He discussed matters of personal hygiene and reprimanded them for spitting on the streets. Agnes's father had a thick Jiangbei accent, and students often laughed when they heard him speak for the first time.

When Agnes was eleven, her mother was hospitalized after jumping off a two-story building and breaking her hand. The following Monday, her father opened his mouth in front of the student assembly, but no words came out, only a moaning sound. He covered his eyes with a fluttering hand. Immediately a collection was started among students and faculty, a generous sum of money raised to pay for her mother's hospital bill. A story was posted on the school's newspaper wall in the courtyard in which a student praised Agnes's father for his selfless devotion to "a walking ghost." Older girls came up to Agnes and pressed her hand. "Your poor mother!" they exclaimed in sad tones. They marveled at her father's goodness, assuring her that a kinder man could not be found.

Agnes intentionally flunked her entrance exams the next year so that she would not have to attend her father's school. She ended up going to a lesser school that was a half-hour commute by bus. Sometimes she rode her old bicycle in order to save bus fare.

Her family occupied a three-room house without running water in the school's outer courtyard. Because her mother was sick, a maid came every week to tidy up their rooms and wash their clothes. The school's kitchen was only twenty yards away, and Agnes washed her face in the same cement basin where the vegetables were rinsed. Her father paid the cook a small sum to prepare their meals, which were always delivered to them covered with an overturned plate. At night they used candles during scheduled blackouts, and, with the exception of her mother, who slept on a narrow bed surrounded by mosquito netting, everyone—her father, her brother, and Agnes—slept on tatami floors.

Sometimes when Agnes mentions her early life in Taiwan to her daughters, they look at her in astonishment, as if she had lived by herself on a deserted island. "That was the nineteen fifties, right?" one of them asks. The other says, "You were so poor!"

"It wasn't so bad," Agnes replies. "Everyone lived the same way, so you didn't notice."

What she remembers most from that time was following a boy in her choir whom she had a crush on. When she passed by him on her bicycle and the wind lifted her skirt, she was in no hurry to pull it down again. Some days, she picked up the cigarette butt that he tossed on the street and slipped the bittersweet end between her lips. She kept a diary, and it was a relief to write down her feelings, but she burned the pages a few years later when not even the handwriting seemed to be her own. She did not want a record to exist. No one in the world would know she had suffered. Agnes thinks now of that girl bicycling around the city, obsessed and burdened by love. It isn't surprising that she never once suspected her father of having a secret life of his own.

Her parents moved to the United States after her father's retirement, and for nine years they lived in their own house in Bloomington, Indiana, a few miles from her brother's farm. After her mother's death, Agnes thought her father would be lonely by himself in the suburbs and suggested that he move to

Washington, DC, to be closer to her and her daughters. She was a part-time real-estate agent (she made most of her money selling life insurance), and she knew of a government-subsidized apartment building in Chinatown for senior citizens. At Evergreen House, he could socialize with people his age, and when he stepped out of his apartment, he had to walk only a couple of blocks to buy his groceries and a Chinese newspaper.

Her father eagerly agreed to this plan. Six months after her mother died, he moved into Evergreen House and quickly made friends with the other residents, playing mahjong twice a week, and even going to church, though he had never been religious before. For lunch, he usually waited in line at the nearby Washington Urban League Senior Center, where he could get a full hot meal for only a dollar.

At seventy-eight, her father looked much the same as he did in Taiwan when Agnes was growing up. For as long as she could remember, her father had been completely bald except for a sparse patch of hair that clung to the back of his head. By the time he was sixty, this shadowy tuft had disappeared, leaving nothing but shiny brown skin like fine, smooth leather. Her father had always been proud of his baldness. "We're more vigorous," he liked to say, "because of our hormones." He reassured Agnes that he would live to a hundred at least.

Every day, her father dressed impeccably in a suit and tie, the same attire that he wore as a principal, even though there was no longer any need for him to dress formally. "Such a gentleman!" Agnes's friends remarked when they saw him. He gazed at them with tranquillity, though Agnes suspected he knew they were saying flattering things about him. His eyes were good-humored, clear, and benign, the irises circled with a pale ring of blue.

If anything, Agnes thought, her father's looks had improved with age. His hollow cheeks had filled out, and he had taken to wearing a fedora with a red feather stuck in the brim, which gave him a charming and dapper air. Maybe, too, it was because he now wore a set of false teeth, which corrected his overbite.

Every other weekend, he took the Metro from his place in Chinatown to Dunn Loring, where Agnes waited for him in her car. He would smile at Agnes as if he hadn't seen her for a year, or as if their meeting were purely a matter of chance and not something they had arranged by telephone. If her teenage daughters were in the car, he would greet them in English. "Hello! How are you?" he said, beaming.

Her daughters laughed. "Fine! And how are you?" they replied.

"Fine!" he exclaimed.

"Good!" they responded.

"Good!" he repeated.

Agnes supposed the three of them found it amusing, their lack of words, their inability to express anything more subtle or pressing to each other. Her daughters were always delighted to see him. They took him out shopping and invited him to the movies. They were good-natured, happy girls, if spoiled and a little careless. Every summer, they visited their father in Florida, and when they came back, their suitcases were stuffed with gifts—new clothes and pretty things for their hair, stuffed animals and cheap bits of jewelry, which they wore for a week and then grew tired of. Their short attention spans sometimes made Agnes feel sorry for her ex-husband, and she enjoyed this feeling of pity in herself very much.

•   •   •

In March, her father visited a former student of his in San Francisco. He came back two weeks later overflowing with health and good spirits. He gave silk purses to the girls and a bottle of Guerlain perfume to Agnes. It was unlike her father to give her perfume, much less one from Paris. She asked him how he had chosen it. "A kind lady helped me," he replied soberly. Agnes thought he meant a saleslady at the store. But later, as she was going through his suit pockets, emptying them of loose change and crumpled tissues and soft pads of lint—she planned on going to the dry cleaner that afternoon—she found a sliver of light blue paper folded into eighths. It was a rough draft of a letter, without a date or signature, addressed to a woman named Qiulian. Her father wrote in a quaint, tipsy hand. His characters were neat though cramped, etched on the page, as the ink from his pen was running out.

You cannot know how happy I was to receive your letter. I hope you are well in San Francisco, and that you have had restful days. I think of you often, perhaps more than I should. Like this morning, for instance, I wondered when exactly you had lived in Nanjing. Is it possible we lived in that city at the same time? I like to think that we passed each other on the street, I, a young man in his early thirties, and you, a schoolgirl in uniform with your hair cut just below the ear. We walked past each other, not knowing our paths would cross again—so many years later!

The cherry trees are in bloom here along the Potomac. I often find myself conversing with you in my head. Look at the falling blossoms, I say. Beautiful, yes? Some people, I know, don't have the courage for anything, but what is there to be afraid of? I thought I would spend the rest of my days alone.

*I can't help but think of the poet Meng Chiao. "Who says
that all things flower in spring?"*

A few characters had been blotted out, a phrase added between
the vertical lines of script. Agnes couldn't help but laugh, even
though there was a slight bitterness in it. How ridiculous that
her father should be courting someone across the country. To
be thinking of love when he should be thinking of the grave.
She called up Hu Tingjun, her father's student in California.
"So who is this Qiulian?" she demanded when he picked up
the phone.

"Ah!" Tingjun said, his voice wavering. He had always
been a little afraid of her since that time she had thrown a glass
of water in his face. But he had a loose tongue, and Agnes
knew he would not be able to resist the urge to gossip. "A real
beauty from the mainland," he declared. "Your father has good
taste."

Agnes allowed this remark to pass without comment. "And
why is she so interested in my father? He doesn't have any
money."

Tingjun laughed. "You underestimate your father's charms."
He paused, and Agnes could hear him sucking his teeth. "I
think she's had a sad life. You know what they say—every
beauty has a tragic story."

Agnes frowned, switching the phone to her other ear.

"Her husband was an art history professor at Nanjing University," Tingjun said. "Struggled against, of course, and died
in a reeducation camp. She married a second time, but this
husband turned out to be a violent character—he beat her, I'm
told, and she divorced him after a few years. She has two children from her first marriage, both of them in Guangzhou. She

came here on a tourist's visa and is staying with an old friend from college."

"So she's been married twice already," Agnes said, "and wants to marry again. She doesn't have a very good track record."

"Have a heart, Shuling. What's so wrong with your father finding comfort in his last days? It's no good to be alone. No good at all."

"I never thought you were a sentimentalist," she said. "I wish I could hand you some tissues!"

Tingjun sighed. "You're always the same, Shuling."

When Agnes hung up the phone, she couldn't help but think of her mother, whom she had always loved more than she loved her father, just as you love something more because it is broken. Her mother had lived to the age of seventy-one, longer than anyone had believed possible, defying the prognostications of doctors, the resignation of her children, and even her own will. Her father had never murmured a word of complaint in all the years he cared for her. In the mornings, he prepared a breakfast for her of pureed apples or boiled carrots. At night he brought her three pills—one sleeping capsule, two that he had filled with sugar—and a tall glass of prune juice. Everything her mother ate had to go into a blender first. She chewed the same mouthful over and over again with slow awareness, sometimes falling asleep with the food still in her mouth. She once told Agnes that every bite she swallowed was like swallowing a small stone. The only thing she enjoyed putting in her mouth were her sleeping pills, and these she swallowed all at once without a sip of water. Perhaps Agnes respected this sickness in her mother more than she did her father's health, his natural exuberance, and his penchant for histrionics.

The day before her mother's funeral, Agnes remembered, she and her brother had gone to a store to look for watches. They had selected a gold watch with a round face, and her brother had asked the salesclerk if there was a warranty, which struck Agnes as funny because the watch was going on her mother's wrist. "Who cares whether it runs beneath the ground or not?" she said. Nevertheless, her mother had always liked to wear a watch. They bought it for her because her old one was broken.

Then Agnes saw her mother lying in her coffin, the new gold watch ticking on her wrist. The sight of her mother lying in such a composed state, looking more content and peaceful than she did when she was alive, made Agnes desperate. She brushed her mother's cheeks and smoothed out her hair with increasing violence, clutching her hand and kissing her cold lips, all the while smelling her powder and the undertaker's handiwork beneath the cloying scent of lilies.

At the funeral reception, her father positioned himself on a stool at the front door of his house so that anyone who passed by had to confront him. At one point, he sprang off his stool and ran across the yard to speak to his neighbor, who had just come home from the store and was holding a bag of groceries. Agnes watched as her father waved his arms, his new suit a size too large for him, the cuffs dangling over his hands and flapping about his wrists. He squeezed his eyes and cried like a child, beating the side of his head with his palm. His neighbor set her bag down, took his hand between her own, and nodded in sympathy, even though she could not understand a word he was saying. Agnes's brother finally intervened, leading their father away so that the neighbor could go inside her house.

"Try to control yourself," Agnes told her father.

"You don't know what it's like to lose someone you saw every day of your life," he said, wiping his eyes.

When the reception was over, after the visitors had departed and her father had shut himself up in his bedroom, Agnes and her brother stood in the backyard, looking at their father's garden.

"The two of them lived in their own world together," her brother said.

Agnes looked at the glossy tomatoes that hung like ornaments from the vines. The winter melons sprawled on the grass like pale, overfed whales. Above them, the sunflowers rose, their faces somehow human, leaning from their stalks. For the first time, she wondered about her parents, the quiet life they had lived in that home.

Agnes never asked her father about the letter she found. In October, he informed her that Qiulian would be flying down in a month and that they would be married in a civil ceremony at the courthouse. He wondered if Agnes would be their witness. Also if there was a restaurant in the area suitable for a small wedding banquet. No more than three tables, he said.

In the marriage bureau, tiny pictures in pastel frames—a cheetah running, an eagle spreading its wings—decorated the walls of the waiting area. There was a sign in the room prohibiting photographs. Agnes sighed as she looked at her watch. Her daughters would be home from school in an hour and would be catching a ride to the banquet with Agnes's friend. Her brother wasn't coming. He had been depressed by their father's news and told Agnes it was too difficult for him to leave the farm. Agnes got up from her seat and inspected a picture of a sailboat skimming moonlit waters. The caption read: *You cannot discover new oceans unless you have the courage to lose sight of the shore.* It made Agnes laugh out loud, and the receptionist glanced up at her from her desk.

Her father arrived a moment later with his bride. He was beaming, handsomely dressed in a dark gray suit and platinum tie, two red carnations fastened to his lapel. He introduced Agnes and Qiulian with mock solemnity, exaggerating the tones of their names, lifting himself in the air and falling back on his heels. Qiulian smiled and told Agnes that her American name was Lily. Everything Lily wore was white. There was her opaque white dress suit with its faintly puffed sleeves. Her pearl earrings and two strands of pearls wound closely around her neck. A corsage of white roses enmeshed in a swirl of white ribbon pinned to her chest. She had decided on white just as if she were a first-time American bride, even though white was no color at all, what you wore to another person's funeral. Perhaps it was a sign of Lily's true feelings.

Agnes grasped her father's arm and pulled him aside. "How old is she, by the way?" It infuriated her that this woman was closer to her age than she had expected.

"That's top secret," her father said, adjusting his carnations. "She's very nice, isn't she? Do I look all right? What do you think of my tie?" He glanced over at Lily, who stood serenely looking at her shoes. She held a small beaded purse between both hands, and it seemed from her empty expression that she was pretending not to hear their conversation. "Incredible!" he muttered. "I'm supposed to feel less as I grow old. But it's the opposite—I feel more and more!" His eyes widened, and he knocked his fist against his chest. "Can you believe it? A seventy-eight-year-old heart like mine!" He walked back to Lily, smiling and patting her hand.

Agnes felt her skin begin to itch. She wanted to lift her

sweater, scratch herself luxuriously until she bled, but the receptionist told them it was time, and they were ushered into a narrow green-carpeted room where the justice of the peace stood waiting behind a podium. Behind him was a trellis on which a few straggling vines of artificial clematis drooped. It was a halfhearted attempt at illusion, and, for this reason, it gave Agnes some relief. It startled her to think that she had once cared about the color of roses matching her bridesmaids' dresses. That day had been a fantasy, with its exquisite bunches of flowers, so perfect they did not seem real. At one point, she had looked up at the sky and laughed . . . she had felt so light and happy. She had worn a white ballroom dress and—of all things—a rhinestone tiara! If photographs still existed of her in that Cinderella outfit, they resided in other people's albums, for she had torn her own into bits.

Her father was listening to the justice with an impassive, dignified expression, his hands folded neatly in front of him. Agnes thought Lily's smile belonged on the face of a porcelain doll. Her hair was cut in short, fashionable waves and seemed ridiculously lustrous for someone her age. Dyed, no doubt. Neither of them understood what the justice was saying, and Agnes had to prompt them when it was time to exchange rings. When the justice pronounced them husband and wife, her father looked around the room, smiling good-naturedly. He thanked the justice with a bow of his head and took Lily gently by the elbow.

Her father visited less often after he was married. The few times he took the subway to Dunn Loring, he did not bring Lily with him. Agnes once asked him why, and he said Lily was quite popular at Evergreen House. "People are always inviting her out to restaurants," he said. "Or she goes over to other ladies' apartments, and they watch the latest Hong Kong melodramas. What sentimental drivel! But she enjoys it, she can't get enough of it . . ." He told Agnes that one day Lily wanted to eat dan dan noodles and nothing but dan dan noodles. "There is a restaurant we know, but the owners were away on vacation. Qiulian suggested another restaurant, but when we got there, it wasn't on the menu and she refused to go inside. She dragged me from one place to another, but none of them served dan dan noodles. I was so hungry by this time, I insisted we go into the next restaurant we saw. But she said she wouldn't eat at all if she couldn't have her dan dan noodles. So we ended up going home, and I had to eat leftovers." Her father shook his head, though he was clearly delighted by Lily's caprice.

From her father, Agnes learned that Lily had studied Chinese history at the prestigious Zhejiang University. She liked to take baths over showers, used Pond's cream on her face at night, and sipped chrysanthemum tea in bed. She rarely bought herself anything, and when she did, the things she chose were charming and fairly priced. Her father gave Lily a monthly allowance of five hundred dollars, which was half the income he received from Agnes and her brother as well as from the federal government. Lily, in turn, sent money to her son, a book vendor, and to her daughter, a truck driver in Guangzhou.

More than a year passed, and Agnes never saw her.

In December, she walked by Lily almost without recognizing her. She had stopped in Chinatown to buy duck for a New Year's Eve party, and a small group of older women approached her on the street. She would not have paid them any attention if the woman in the gray raincoat had not paused to stare in the middle of readjusting a silk scarf around her head. It took Agnes a moment to realize it was Lily. By that time, the women had passed, heading south in the direction of Evergreen House.

Agnes stood on the sidewalk, gazing absently at a faded brick building, its pink paint flaking off to reveal dark red patches. Even in the winter, the streets smelled of grease and the hot air blown out of ventilators. Behind a row of buildings, two looming cranes crisscrossed the sky. It was odd to think of someone like Lily living here. Agnes went inside the restaurant to get her duck, and by the time she stepped outside again, tiny flakes of snow were falling. She did not go back to her car but instead turned in the direction of her father's apartment.

Outside his door, she heard shrill voices and laughter, the noisy clacking of tiles being swirled along a table. The mahjong ladies, Agnes thought. Lily answered the door, her mild, empty eyes widening slightly. Her mass of glossy black hair was perfectly coiffed, and only her wrinkled neck betrayed her age.

"I saw you on the street," Agnes said. "Didn't you see me?"

"Yes," Lily said, pausing. "But I wasn't sure it was you until we had passed each other."

"The same with me." Agnes pulled off her coat and tossed it onto the sofa. "So, who are your friends here?"

"Oh yes, let me introduce you to my neighbors." The mahjong ladies half stood out of their seats, smiling at Agnes, but it was obvious they wanted to return to their game.

"Don't let me disturb you," Agnes told them. "Is my father here?"

"He's taking a nap," Lily said, seating herself at the table.

The living room was brightly lit compared with the dimness of the hallway. It seemed like its own island in space as the afternoon waned and the windows darkened. The mahjong ladies chattered, flinging their tiles to the middle of the table. They were older than Lily, in their seventies at least, their hands plowed with wrinkles, with bright green circles of jade hanging from their wrists. Their fingers, too, were weighed down by gaudy rings, the stones as shiny as candy, purple and turquoise and vermilion. "He ate oatmeal every day," a woman with badly drawn eyebrows was saying.

"I heard he took poison," another said, picking up a tile. She had thick, sour lips and wore red horn-rimmed glasses. "Didn't he lose everything?"

"No, it was a heart attack. His wife found him still sitting on the toilet! In the middle of reading a newspaper."

"He was too cheap to pay for his own funeral," the third one said. She had a sagging, magisterial face, her thick white hair pulled back into a bun. "In his will, he donated his body to science."

The one with the false eyebrows knocked down all of her tiles. "Hula!" she declared.

There were startled cries. "I wasn't even close!"

"Did anyone have three sticks?"

Agnes smiled as she poured herself a cup of tea from the counter. These ladies were real witches, talking about people's ends with such morbid assurance—how could Lily stand their company? Perhaps she liked the attention, for she seemed to be the silent center of the group, the one the ladies exclaimed over and petted. Lily glanced toward Agnes from time to time, smiling at her. She seemed impatient for Agnes to leave.

"Well," Agnes said, after she had finished her tea, "he won't mind too much if I wake him." She walked across the room and opened the bedroom door, even though she sensed this was precisely what Lily did not want her to do.

Her father sat at his desk reading a newspaper, his bifocals slipping down his nose. A single lamp illuminated his down-turned head, and it seemed from his silence that he had been exiled here. His manner changed the moment he saw her. His face broke into an exuberant smile as he stood up from his chair.

"So what are you doing here? Come to pay me a visit?"

Agnes closed the door behind her. "I've brought you a duck," she said. "And to wish you a happy new year."

"A duck? Did you go to the Golden Palace?"

"I did."

"That's the best place to go. They have better ducks than anywhere else. Number one ducks!" he said. "So plump! And with crispy skin."

Agnes looked at her father. "And how are you these days?"

"I'm fine!" he declared. "I'm good! Just look at me." He straightened his argyle sweater over his shirt and tie, then preened in front of the mirror, turning his head to one side and then the other.

"You don't play mahjong with the ladies," she said, looking around the room. The furniture was mismatched—things that she had given him which she no longer had any use for. A chair from an old dining room table set. A desk with buttercup yellow legs. A massive dresser with gothic iron handles. It bothered Agnes to see her daughter's stickers still on one of the drawers.

"You know me. I'm not good at these sorts of games. I'm a scholar, I read things . . . like this newspaper," he said, waving it in the air. "Besides, they want to talk freely without me hanging about."

"What's that doing in here?" Agnes asked. "Is that where she makes you sleep?" In the corner, between the bed and the closet, was a makeshift cot covered with a comforter folded in half like a sleeping bag.

"The bed is too soft on my poor back," her father said. He pressed his hand against his spine and winced. "This way is more comfortable."

Agnes sat down on the thin cot, which bounced lightly. "So this is how she treats you," she said. "She won't even let you into her bed."

"Her sleep isn't good." Her father cleared his throat, setting the newspaper down on his desk. "She often wakes up in the middle of the night." He didn't look at her as he fiddled with the pages, then folded the paper back together. Agnes felt an involuntary stirring in her chest. She had avoided him all this time, not wanting to know about his marriage because she had not wanted to know of his happiness. But she should have known Lily was the kind of person who took care only of herself.

"How else is she behaving?" she asked. "Is she mistreating you in any way?"

"No, no," her father said hurriedly, shaking his head.

"Is she a wife to you?" There was a pause as he looked at her. "You know what I mean," she said.

"She suffers a pain," he offered hesitantly. "In her ovaries."

Agnes laughed. She got up and strode across the room, flinging the door open.

"Don't say anything," her father said, following after her. "Don't let her know what I've told you."

In the living room, the mahjong ladies were laughing and knocking over their walls, and Agnes had to raise her voice above theirs. "I'd like to talk to you," she said to Lily.

For a moment, Lily pretended not to hear, continuing her conversation with the white-haired lady beside her. Then she glanced over at Agnes, her face a mask of porcelain elegance except for one delicately lifted eyebrow. "What is it?"

"Why aren't you sleeping with my father?"

The ladies' voices fell to a murmur, their hands slowing down as they massaged the tiles along the tablecloth. They looked at Lily, who said nothing, though her smile seemed to be sewn on her lips.

Her father clutched Agnes's arm, but she refused to be silent. "You married him, didn't you? He pays for your clothes and your hairdo and this roof over your head. He deserves something in return!"

Her father laughed out loud and immediately put his hand over his mouth.

Lily stood up, but the mahjong ladies remained in their seats as if drunk, their eyes glazed with the thrill of the unexpected. "Perhaps we can resume our games later," Lily said. The one with the horn-rimmed glasses stood up slowly from the table, prompting the other two to rise. They looked as if they had been shaken out of a dream.

"Oh, my heavens!" the one with the eyebrows exclaimed as Agnes shut the door on them.

"Now," Agnes said, turning toward Lily and waiting for her to speak.

"I have an illness . . ." Lily began. "A gynecological disorder that prevents me . . ." Her gaze wandered to Agnes's father, who hovered near the bedroom door. "Well, in truth, he's an old man," she said, her expression hardening. "His breath stinks like an open sewer. I can't stand to smell his breath!" She snatched her scarf from the closet and wrapped it quickly around her head.

"If you don't sleep with him," Agnes said, "I'll send a letter to the immigration office. I'll tell them that you only married him to get a green card!"

Lily's hands trembled as she put on her coat. "Do as you like," she said, walking out the door.

Her father looked deeply pained.

"She won't refuse you now," Agnes told him.

"What has happened?" her father said, his voice shaking. "Who are you? You've become someone . . . someone completely without shame!"

"I should open up a brothel," Agnes declared. "That is exactly what I should do."

In February, her father called to tell her he wasn't sure whether or not his nose was broken. There had been a snowstorm two days before, whole cars sheathed in ice, the roads filled with irregular lumps, oddly smooth and plastic, where the snow had melted and then frozen again. In this weather, her father and Lily had gone out walking to buy groceries at Da Hua Market. Lily had walked ahead, and when she was almost half a block away, she turned around and asked Agnes's father to walk faster. He tried to keep up with her, but corns had formed along his toes and the soles of his feet. When he quickened his pace, he slipped on a deceptively bland patch of ice and hit his nose on the pavement.

When Agnes saw her father—a dark welt on the bridge of his nose, a purple stain beginning to form under his eyes—she couldn't help but feel a flood of anger and pity. You could have lived your last years in peace, she wanted to say to him. Instead she glanced at the closed bedroom door. "Is that where she's hiding?"

He looked at her morosely. "She left earlier because she knew you were coming."

In the hospital, Agnes noticed that her father walked gingerly down the hall, stepping on the balls of his feet without touching his toes or heels to the ground. An X-ray revealed that his nose was not broken after all. Agnes told the resident he was having problems walking.

"That's not an emergency," the resident replied. Nevertheless, she left the room to call in a podiatrist.

Her father grew excited when he saw the podiatrist. He began speaking to him in Chinese.

"I'm sorry," the podiatrist said, shaking his head. "I'm Korean. Let's take these off, shall we?" He lightly pulled off her father's socks. There were red cone-shaped bumps along his toes and hard yellow mounds on the soles and heels of his feet. But what shocked Agnes most was the big toe on his left foot. The nail of this one toe looked a thousand years old to her, thick, encrusted, and wavy, black in the center and as impenetrable as a carapace.

"Older people's toenails are often like this," the podiatrist said, seeing Agnes's surprise.

Her father seemed oblivious to their comments. He was squeezing his eyes shut as the podiatrist worked on his foot, slicing the calluses off bit by bit with a small blade. Her father winced and jerked his feet up occasionally. "Oh, it hurts," he exclaimed to Agnes. "It's unbearable!"

"I know this isn't pleasant," the podiatrist said, looking at her father. He took a pumice stone out of his pocket and rubbed it gently against her father's foot.

When the podiatrist had finished paring away at his corns, her father covered his feet back up, slowly pulling on his socks and tying the laces of his shoes. He smiled at the podiatrist, yet because of his bruised nose, his face seemed pathetic and slightly grotesque. "It's better beyond words," he said.

In the parking lot, her father showed off by walking at a sprightly pace in front of her. "It's so much better now!" he kept exclaiming.

The doctor had told Agnes that the corns would eventually come back, but she didn't tell her father. She was thinking how well he had hidden the signs of old age from her. That big toe underneath his sock. Since the time she was a child, she and her father had lived their lives independent of each other. She had never demanded anything of him, and he had been too busy with his work at school, so that by the time she was six she had been as free as an adult. They left each other alone mostly because of her mother, whose sickness filled up the entire house and whose moods were inextricably bound with their own.

In the car, Agnes told her father that she thought he should divorce Lily.

"It's not as bad as that, Shuling."

"I hate how she humiliates you," she said.

Her father was silent, gazing out the window. "Love is humiliating," he finally replied.

When she dropped him off in front of his building, he did not immediately go inside but stood on the frozen sidewalk, waving at her. She knew he would stay there until her car was no longer in sight. It was his way of seeing her off, and he would do this no matter what the weather.

In June, her father called to see if Agnes had any photographs of his wedding banquet. He and Lily were going to be interviewed by an immigration officer next week in order to secure

Lily's green card, and her father planned to present the photos as evidence. Agnes could find only one photograph. She had dumped it into a shoebox, to be lost in an ever growing stack of useless pictures. Years ago, she had stopped putting her family's photographs in an album. Now whenever their pictures were developed, after her daughters' initial enthusiasm of looking at themselves, Agnes put the photos back into their original envelopes and tossed them into a shoebox.

The photograph she found was of Lily, her father, and two old couples seated at their table. Lily was looking away from the camera, her mouth oddly pursed, as if she were in the middle of chewing her food while smiling at the same time. A pair of chopsticks rested between her fingers. It was an odd moment. Lily appeared sociable yet also removed. Her eyes were lively, though they looked at nothing in particular. It was as if two versions of her had been captured in the same photograph.

Actually, there were two photographs of Lily that Agnes found. Two copies of the same picture. Agnes wanted to find a difference, something very small—a gesture of the hand, the curve of an eyebrow—but the two pictures were exactly alike. Another photograph of Lily would reveal another world. But there she was—Lily could never break out of the picture, an elegant woman caught in the act of chewing. Beside her, her father looked radiant, a little too well satisfied, two red carnations and a wisp of baby's breath pinned right over his heart. He was the only person in the photograph looking at the camera.

"Do you want to come over on Saturday to pick it up?" she asked her father. "You can stay for the weekend, and I'll drive you to your interview on Monday."

Her father hesitated. "You don't have to come in with me. You can just drop me off at the immigration office."

"Fine," Agnes said.

The morning of his interview, her father ironed his own dress shirt and put on a suit that still smelled of the dry cleaner's fumes. He shaved the tiny white hairs that had begun to sprout on his chin, and even sprayed himself with an old bottle of cologne that he found in a bathroom drawer. An hour before his appointment, he began to fidget, looking at his watch and pacing around the room. "Shouldn't we be leaving?" he asked.

"Sit down. We have plenty of time."

"I don't want to be late," he said, picking up his bag. "Qiu-lian will be waiting."

Agnes sat down, tapping a pack of cigarettes in her hand. Smoking was one of the bad habits she blamed on her father, even though he had quit twenty years ago. "You realize, don't you," Agnes said, blowing smoke to the side away from him. "It's a certain fact. She'll leave you as soon as she gets her green card."

Her father cleared his throat and switched the bag to his other hand.

"You want her to stay, am I right?"

He sighed, heading toward the door. "Let's not talk about this anymore."

"I'm not taking you," she said. She flicked the ash off her cigarette onto a plate. "It's for your own good. I won't let her have it."

Her father shook his head. "Unbelievable," he said.

"I wrote a letter to the INS already. In the letter, I informed them that your marriage — your wife — is a fraud."

Her father closed his eyes, shaking his head. He began breathing heavily and grasped his collar.

"What would Mother say?" she said. "You were such an easy dupe!"

"You and her!" he said, looking at Agnes. "You make me want to die!" He hit his palm twice against his forehead. "I want to die!"

"You were so eager to jump into another woman's bed," Agnes said. "But you didn't know she wouldn't let you touch her. Not even if you married her!"

"A dirty old man," her father laughed. "Yes, I am a dirty old man! I sleep with whoever I want! I slept with our maids, you know that? It only cost a few dollars each time! Sometimes I did it when you were in the house, and you never knew. It was like you were knocked out, and I wondered if you took your mother's sleeping pills. Because you never knew! You never knew!" He was talking so fast that spittle was forming on his lips.

Agnes felt her throat burning and tried to swallow.

"I slept with all of them!" her father repeated.

"I don't believe you."

"Yes!"

"Those women? They were old and fat—"

"Who cares? Their bodies were warm."

"Disgusting."

"Yes, everything is disgusting to you." Her father walked to the front door.

"Where do you think you're going?" she screamed.

He left the door open, and she watched him walk down the driveway with a jaunty step. She wondered if he knew how to get out of the neighborhood. It was still morning, but the humidity was unbearable. She picked up the newspaper lying on the doorstep and went back inside. She would let him walk as much as he wanted. It would serve him right if he got heatstroke.

At eleven, the phone rang. It was Lily, waiting at the INS and wondering where her father was. "He won't be able to make it," Agnes said, and she hung up the phone. But she felt herself shaking. Wasn't it obvious, wasn't it to be expected—a healthy, vital man married to an invalid for over forty years? And yet, she had never suspected. She remembered the speeches he gave, how everyone had called him a gentleman . . . and it was not what he had done that disturbed her so much as her own sickening ignorance. She felt as if a hole had opened up inside her chest, all the things she had known and believed slipping through.

Another hour passed, and still her father had not returned. What if he should simply lie down and die like a dog in the street? The thought made Agnes leave her house. She drove around her neighborhood, turning down streets that ended in culs-de-sac. She felt something round and heavy inside her forehead, as if it were splitting open from the heat. She turned out of her neighborhood onto a narrow two-lane road that dipped and curved without warning, and she couldn't help but feel dread growing inside her, a darkness that she wanted to make small again, half expecting to see her father lying on the side of the road.

She spotted him three miles farther down. He was walking at a much slower pace with his jacket along his arm. He had loosened his tie, and his white shirt was semitransparent with sweat. She slowed down and honked at him, but he kept trudging ahead, without turning to look at her. Agnes rolled down the passenger window. "Get in the car," she said, but he began to walk faster, with small, clumsy steps. He was panting and bobbing his head with each stride, intent on pressing forward, even though she knew his feet must be hurting him.

"It's useless to walk," she said, driving slowly beside him. "How far are you going to get, huh? Don't be foolish. Get in the car."

He shook his head, and she could see that he was crying.

"I'll take you back to your apartment. I promise, okay?"

He walked more slowly now, and she felt sorry for him, knowing there was nothing for him to do but give in. When she got out of the car, he was standing motionless, his arms hanging at his sides and his jacket on the ground. She touched his arm, and he blinked, looking around in bewilderment as she helped him into the car.

He began shivering as soon as he sat down in the passenger seat, and Agnes turned down the air-conditioning. Neither of them spoke as Agnes drove to his apartment. At Evergreen House, he hurriedly got out of the car, searching his pockets for his keys. Agnes realized that they had forgotten to get his bag at her house. Nevertheless, the security guard recognized him and let him inside the building.

When Agnes was twenty-two, she left Taiwan to study economics in Rochester, New York. She left her home and her parents with a feeling of relief. Her family life had become a source of embarrassment to her, and as her plane lifted into the air—it was the first time she had ever flown—she felt that she was abandoning an idea of herself. She looked outside her window, the things she knew shrinking steadily away until all she could see were clouds, and she welcomed the prospect of being unknown in another part of the world.

In Rochester, she received a blue rectangle of a letter every other week from her father in Taiwan. On the front, he would write out her address in English with a painstaking, scrupulous hand. He told her about the vegetables he was growing in the courtyard, the Siamese cat that Agnes had left in their care, the state of her mother's health and the various foods she could keep down, news of her brother in the army, and updates of their relatives and friends, some of whom were leaving for the States. She would write back, sometimes enclosing a money order for twenty dollars. She could not afford to call them on the phone, but the few times she did, she heard her own voice echoing along the line, a high, unfamiliar sound, and this distracted her, made her think of all the distance her voice had to cross to reach their ears. Her parents always asked the same questions—*How are you? Are you eating well? Are you happy?*—until the static took over and their voices ended abruptly. Listening to the silence, she imagined their voices being dropped from a high space into the ocean.

She sent her parents a hateful letter once. They had set a date for her brother's wedding without consulting her, and it enraged Agnes to find out that she would not be able to attend. The next letter she received came from her mother, who rarely wrote after her fall. Her handwriting resembled the large uncontrolled scrawl of a child or of someone who was righthanded trying to use her left. She had copied Agnes's address so poorly that it was a miracle the letter had arrived at all. *We received your letter in which you scolded us severely. Your father fainted after reading it, and it took him a long time before he could eat his dinner. He has heart trouble and cannot suffer any blows.* At the time, Agnes had been amused by her mother's lies. Her father had no history of heart trouble, and as for his fainting, she knew what a good actor he was. But it was her mother's last phrase that had come to haunt her. *He . . . cannot suffer any blows.*

Agnes did not hear from her father for over a month, and in that time she felt as removed from him as if he were living in another country. One day in August, she stopped by his apartment to give him a box of persimmons. Lily answered the door in gray slacks and a thin, watery blouse, a silk scarf wrapped around her head as if she were about to go out. "He's not here," she said coldly, and began to shut the door.

"Wait—" Agnes said, putting her hand out.

Lily held the door open only wide enough for her face to be visible. The powder she wore could not quite hide the fine lines etched beneath her eyes, nor the age spots above her cheeks.

"Do you know when he'll be back?" Agnes asked.

"I have no idea."

"I'd like to wait for him if you don't mind."

"Wait for as long as you like," Lily said, turning away. She retreated to her bedroom and closed the door.

Agnes set the persimmons on the kitchen counter. Her father had hung red and gold New Year's greeting cards from the slats of the closet door. In the living room, he had decorated the walls with whimsical scrolled paintings of fruit and birds. She had always been somewhat relieved by his attempts to make the place more livable. Perhaps she was trying to console herself for the drab carpet and clumsy furniture, the sense of apology she always felt for things that were merely adequate. After two years, there was hardly any trace of Lily in the apartment, but this didn't surprise Agnes, as Lily had never intended to stay for long.

She paused outside the bedroom door before knocking. "I'd like to talk to you," she said.

"Come in, then," a voice evenly replied.

Agnes saw Lily sitting on the side of her bed, a ghostly smile on her lips as she studied the scarf in her hands. She seemed like another person to Agnes, ten or fifteen years older at least, and it took a moment for Agnes to realize that her beautiful, shiny black hair was gone. Instead, wisps of ash-colored hair were matted together in places like dead grass. The sparseness of her hair revealed mottled patches of scalp.

"What happened?" Agnes blurted. She couldn't help but stare at Lily's baldness.

"You didn't know?" Lily said. She touched her head lightly with a flat hand, her eyes vacant as she smiled to herself. "When I was struggled against, they pulled my hair out by the fistfuls, and it never grew back again. You would think it would grow back, but it doesn't always."

Agnes was silent for a moment. "Hu Tingjun told me about your first husband," she said.

"My first husband," Lily echoed, and it seemed to Agnes as if those words had lost their meaning to her. "Yes, my first husband was an avid collector of calligraphy. Did you know he had a work by Zhu Yunming that was more than four hundred years old? He said the characters flowed on the paper like a flight of birds. Like a wind was lifting them off the page."

Agnes shook her head. "I don't know much about calligraphy."

"This work was more than four hundred years old," Lily said, "can you imagine? My husband begged them not to destroy it. 'I'll give it to the state!' he said. But they said, 'Why would the state want such an old thing?' And they burned it before his eyes. Sometimes I wish I could tell him, 'Is someone's handwriting worth more than your life?' I would have burned a hundred such pieces. You see, I'm not an idealistic person. There are things one must do out of necessity."

"My father is a foolish man," Agnes said.

Lily looked at her, twisting the scarf between her fingers.

"Yet it's impossible to hate him. He doesn't have any cruelty in him."

"So you have your green card now."

"A few more months," Lily said.

"Where will you go after this?"

"California. My son is living there now."

"Does my father know?"

Lily nodded, dropping the scarf on the night table. "He's afraid, you see." She lay down on the bed, folding her hands over her stomach, her feet sheathed in brown panty hose. "He knows his mind is fading, but he won't admit it. He shouldn't be allowed to live by himself for too long." Lily closed her eyes. "I once told myself that I'd be happy, I'd never complain, if only I was safe. But I'm so tired of living here. I can't tell you how bored I am!" She curled up on her side, placed both hands underneath her cheek. "Do you mind turning off the light as you go out? I'm going to take a little nap now. It seems all I can do is sleep." She murmured her thanks as Agnes left the room, closing the door behind her.

Her father never mentioned Lily's departure, nor did Agnes say anything, both of them lapsing into a silence that seemed to make Lily more present in the room, just as her mother was often there in the room between them, in the air they breathed and the words they did not say.

One night, while her father was visiting, Agnes woke to find the light still on in his bedroom. When she knocked on his door, she saw that he was dressed in his suit and tie, his bags already packed, even though it was only two in the morning. She told him to go back to sleep, that it was still too early, and he smiled at her, waving from behind his ear as he closed the door. She stood in the hallway, and after a moment he turned off his light, but she knew he was sitting in the dark, waiting.

In January, the manager of Evergreen House called Agnes to inform her that her father had stopped paying the rent. "He gets confused," the manager said. "Sometimes he doesn't recognize us."

Her father laughed when Agnes asked him about the rent. "Nobody pays rent here," he replied. Then he told her he suspected the manager of being a thief. "If anything happens to me, you should know that I have a hiding place for my cash. There's a brick in the wall which can be removed."

Agnes and her brother agreed that it was time for their father to live with one of them. Their father didn't offer a word of protest. An airplane ticket to Indiana was purchased, and one weekend in February Agnes went over to his apartment to help pack his things.

He answered the door in his slippers. The television was on, and he was watching a basketball game. His apartment smelled musty, like old newspapers. Perhaps it was the wood paneling or the brown carpet worn as soft as moss. The sick sweetness emanated from deep within the wood. The carpet had inhaled odors that had been pressed in for years by slippered feet.

She took a suitcase out of his closet and packed it hastily without too much folding. She did not like the intimacy of touching his clothes, as if he were already dead. He hung vaguely about her for a few minutes, then wandered out of the room. In a short while, he came back, looking around as if he were trying to find something. "What are you looking for?" she asked him.

He shook his head, closing his eyes, then left the room.

She finished packing two of his suitcases and dragged them to the front door. She found him standing on his balcony, watching a plane as it flew over the building. "That's the ninth one today," he said when she looked at him.

"You tell me what else you want to bring, and I'll send it to you."

"What's the use?" he said. "I don't need anything here. I probably won't live to see another year."

"Don't be so self-pitying," she told him.

In the elevator, an old man stood in the corner, both hands leaning against his walking stick. "Mr. Cao," her father said, smiling suddenly. "How are you? Let me introduce you to my wife."

"I'm not your wife," Agnes said, irritated. "I'm your daughter."

Her father screwed up his eyes, his fingers digging into his temple. Then he let out a loud, embarrassed laugh. Yet he seemed delighted by his mistake. "My daughter," he said. "Please excuse me. Yes, of course, my daughter."

After she saw off her father at the airport, Agnes remembered the secret place he had told her about where he had hidden his money, and she decided to return to his apartment.

In the living room, she stared at the scrolled paintings on the wall. Melons with their curling vines, a powder blue bird hanging on a branch too thin for its talons, a lopsided horse as fat as a cow scratching its neck against a tree. She took these scrolls off their hooks and rolled them up. Then she ran her hand along the wall, searching for a loose brick. She could not find one. She pressed her hands against the bricks until the skin on her palms tingled with rawness. Anyone who saw her grop-ing this way would think she was mad.

She looked in his desk drawers and underneath his mattress. She crawled around trying to find a loose spot in the carpet, but there was no part that would come undone. She could almost swear the carpet smelled faintly carcinogenic. Had he smoked a cigarette here? Maybe, after all, it was a habit he couldn't leave behind.

In his closet, she found a door to a crawl space that had been hidden by his clothes. She had to crouch through to get in. It was a place for storage and apparently had never been swept, the floor littered with sawdust. She couldn't see much of anything and went back for a lamp, which she left in the closet as far as the cord could reach. There was nothing in the space except an old crumpled shirt, which she knew was not her father's. But then in the dim recess where the light barely reached, she saw a yellow shape, which turned out to be a suitcase, and just looking at it she knew it was her father's, something her parents had used when they still lived in Taiwan. The suitcase lay on its side, and there were gashes in the fabric which he had covered up with duct tape.

Agnes sneezed twice when she unzipped the suitcase. She expected old clothes, maybe even the cash he had mentioned, but instead the suitcase was crammed full of letters. The envelopes were cold to the touch, permeated with the chill dankness of the room, as cold as a basement. Her father had thrown them in rather heedlessly, and the letters had conformed to the shape of each other. She could see this in the indentations of the envelopes, pressed and stuck together like so many leaves. Little rectangles of blue paper, with red and blue stripes along the borders. *Aérogramme. Par avion.* There were long, slender envelopes with torn sides, the corners cut out with scissors where the stamps had been. She recognized some of the names on the envelopes—Jia Wen, Wang Peisan, Zhou Meiping, Wu Yenchiu—various friends and colleagues of her father's, though she was unsure if any of them were still living.

In the pile, she spotted her own handwriting. A letter she had written to her father from Rochester. She had always been careless about her writing, and her characters now struck her as hasty and anonymous in their uniformity. She put the letter aside and searched through the pile for her mother's name. She felt a strange sensation similar to the hope she felt whenever she saw her mother in her dreams. The envelope she reached for was covered with tea-colored stains, fantastically bent, curling around the edges. Though her mother's name was on the front, the handwriting was unfamiliar to Agnes. She pulled out a tissue-thin sheet of rice paper, folded vertically in thirds. The letter was dated February 19, 1946. Her mother wrote with a strong, fluid hand.

I have arrived safely in Yancheng. The doll you gave Shuling is quite beautiful and interesting. She is always playing with it, holding it in her hands, and I'm afraid she'll break it, so I put it in a glass jar so that she can look but not touch. Let her appreciate it more that way. Her appetite has improved lately. You would be amazed to see how quickly she moves about, how she turns left and right as she walks. She tries to talk, and I still don't understand her, but her hands point to different things, and I know what she wants.

Agnes couldn't finish the letter and slipped it back into its envelope. Better to forget, she told herself. Her fingers smelled of dust and old paper, and she stared vacantly at the suitcase full of letters. Had he left them behind for her? She wished she had never found them. On all the envelopes, his name. Hsu

Weimin. Addresses she had forgotten and others she had never known. All the places he had ever lived. Yancheng and Hechuan and Nanjing and Taipei. Then the last places. Bloomington. Washington, DC.

Agnes stood up, wiping the dust off her fingers. In the kitchen, she found an empty trash bag, and she returned to the crawl space, grabbing letters by the fistful and throwing them inside. How cold and brittle they were! She would never read them, she knew that, and their presence was a small stone in her heart. Nothing lasts, and she was not a sentimental person.

"You cannot blame me," she said out loud, as if her father were in the room, watching.

Somewhere in the sky, her father lives. Perhaps he is asleep, perhaps looking out of his window, the clouds washing past in a dizzying blur of motion. In the rush of the plane, does he too sense that there is nowhere for him to go?

A VISIT TO THE SUNS

June was waiting inside one of the terminals at the Los Angeles airport. Her uncle had called to say he was stuck in traffic and would be an hour late, and she opened up a newspaper that someone had left behind on the seat beside her. The newspaper, the *Mainichi Daily News,* was one she had never heard of. She flipped through the pages and began reading an article about *hikikomori,* socially alienated youth who rarely come out of their rooms. Apparently there had been a disturbing case of one *hikikomori* who abducted a nine-year-old girl at knifepoint and forced her into the trunk of his car. He kept the girl in his bedroom for the next nine years without his mother knowing, even though she lived in the same house.

The man, Nobuyuki Sato, had wrapped adhesive tape around the girl's hands and feet at first, then trained her to speak quietly, not to touch the door or get off the bed without his permission. Whenever she disobeyed, he punched her or used a stun gun on her arms and legs. After a while, the girl lost her will to escape. She said she felt as though she were tied up with invisible tape, and she stayed in the room even when Sato left the house without locking the door. As there was little she was allowed to do, the girl said she stepped on the bed in order to feel alive. She was found in a sleeping bag by health officials called in by Sato's mother. The mother didn't know who the girl was and said she hadn't been allowed in her son's room for over twenty years. The girl had been starved and was too weak to get out of the bag by herself. She didn't want to cross over the red tape Sato had placed on the floor in the shape of a box and asked the officials to let her stay where she was.

June felt a little sick after reading the article and was glad to set the newspaper aside. She wandered around the terminal and went inside a gift shop, where she bought a bottle of Johnnie Walker for her uncle, even though he probably wouldn't drink it, and a box of chocolates for her cousins. Then she found a restroom and rinsed her face with cold water. By the time she stepped outside, almost an hour had passed, and she hoped her uncle would come soon. She thought once more about the girl, Fusako Sano, and what she had said about stepping on the bed in order to feel alive.

According to the article, most *hikikomori* were not violent. That was a relief, as June couldn't help but think of her younger brother in college. He was no psychopath, of course, but it was always a struggle to get him out of his room. The few times she saw him each year, when both of them were home for the holidays, he seemed to exist solely in front of his computer. He stayed awake until the wee hours playing an online game in which he assumed the role of a sorcerer who could breathe underwater and had a pet cockroach. Their mother delivered food to him on a tray, and when June berated her for spoiling him, her mother was quick to defend herself. "If I don't bring food up to him, he'll eat junk food," she said. "Or nothing at all!"

A few times June had burst into his room and tried to drag him out of bed by pulling on his arm. "We're going to a restaurant, don't you want to come?" But he only wrapped the blanket tighter around himself, sealing his body in an impenetrable cocoon and refusing to open his eyes. When he was a child, he had sought her out every evening because he was bored or lonely. She was nine years older than he, busy with school and her own friends, and when he knocked on her door, she often considered him a nuisance and told him to go away. She relented sometimes when he asked her to read to him, but she knew he didn't really care about the books and only wanted to be close to her. She had never been able to get him to read on his own.

The last time June was home was in December, four months ago. During that visit, her mother had entreated her brother, "Do not become like your pet gerbil!" This gerbil had always been cared for by June's mother and lived a circumscribed life in the corner of the laundry room, often gnawing on the bars of its cage. June felt sorry for it and gave it newspaper to shred, but her mother claimed the ink was bad for its teeth. June had bought a wheel for it to run on, but the rodent was too stupid to exercise. It ate and grew fat and nested beneath tissue paper and pine shavings, and June could not imagine a more pitiful, monotonous life.

A quarter of an hour passed before she saw a blue van pull up onto the curb. A thin, graying man with a receding brow sprang out of the driver's seat and approached her. His eyes were startled, not resting on anything in particular, and he kept craning his neck and looking around him. She smiled, but he gave no sign that he recognized her.

"Hello, Uncle," she said.

He stared at her for a moment and seemed overwhelmed by

his own thoughts. "That all you have—nothing more?" he asked her.

"That's it," she replied. "This is for you." She gave him the plastic bag with the liquor and chocolates, and he nodded without looking at what was inside. When he seized the other bag she was carrying, she tried to resist out of politeness, but he had a wiry grip and finally she had to let go.

The back of her uncle's van was cluttered with a stack of newspapers, half-opened boxes of the merchandise he sold, mostly pens and watches, and cardboard trays of iced coffee and fruit drinks. He cleared a space for her bag and handed her a warm can of mango juice. "You like?" he said. June thanked him and took a seat in front. He had covered all the seats with tattered straw mats to protect the fabric, and, besides being uncomfortable to sit on, they made the van seem shabbier than it was.

Her uncle was silent until they reached the highway. Then he smiled through clenched teeth, his eyes darting over at her. "June, you talk to Helen, okay?"

"Yes, of course, Uncle."

He sighed. "You talk to her, right? Helen's mind not so good." He rapped the side of his head with his knuckles. "She isn't like you, right? Your father said Ph.D. at Berkeley!"

"Actually, I'm only getting a master's."

"You know Helen failed two courses last term? You know how we find out? Her roommate told us. Helen is lying to us for a year now. Her mother and I are . . . how do you say it? We are *tongku.*" His hand fluttered over his chest. "Brokenhearted. Very sad hearts. Maybe she lose her scholarship. It's because she's involved in this crazy . . . what do you call it? What's the word?" A car honked at him as he swerved into the other lane.

"A cult?" June said, buckling her seat belt. She had already heard the story from her parents.

"These people! They see you lonely, and say, 'We are your friend.' And Helen feels — she wants to help them, right? — and they . . . what you call it? *Xi nao.*"

"Brainwash?"

"Brainwash, yes. And she writes a check! They wash her brain, and she writes a check!" He broke into sharp laughter. "You religious?" June shook her head. "You strong, right?" her uncle said, making a fist. "I say to Helen these people aren't your true friend. You can trust me, your mother, your cousin with a Ph.D. Because we are family, and only family is your true friend."

June didn't know what to say to this. The last time she saw Helen was almost ten years ago, when her uncle's family spent Christmas at her parents' home in Washington, DC. Helen was a quiet, withdrawn girl with long, shadowy hair who didn't seem to mind that her own parents ignored her and doted instead on her younger brother, Gerard. Helen wasn't pretty — her eyes were too small, her nose too big, and she had inherited her mother's thick lips — but she was gentle and serious, which June appreciated and thought unusual for a child.

According to June's mother, Helen had come out of the library one afternoon and been approached by a young Korean woman who had given her a pamphlet. And Helen had gone to one of the services by herself and now wore a tiny silver cross around her neck. Her parents didn't mind at first that their daughter had found Jesus Christ. The people Helen associated with were polite, neatly dressed, and spoke with melodious voices. It was hard not to be impressed by their calm spiritual glow. The young women were especially beautiful with their clear moon faces and wore no makeup to show off their luminous complexions. Everything seemed okay until Helen's roommate, a short Taiwanese girl who had been her best friend since high school, arrived on their doorstep with a scowling, tragic face. She had come unwillingly, forced and accompanied by her parents, who insisted that she tell the Suns all that was happening to Helen.

It seemed that every moment of Helen's life was taken up by her new church, and her roommate hardly saw her anymore. In the evenings there was devotion time, Bible study, prayer meetings. On the weekends, besides worship, there were picnics, retreats, dinners, bowling, puppet shows, church skits, and singing. Helen was always baking cupcakes. When the group found out that Helen was artistic, they asked her to make handmade cards for all the people leaving on missions. She was discouraged from associating with nonbelievers except for the sole purpose of ministering to them. The roommate felt that the church had taken Helen away from her and bitterly complained to her parents about it. Of course, her parents would not have interfered, they told the Suns, in an ordinary falling-out between friends. But their daughter had said Helen was failing her classes and giving away all her savings to the church.

"What we give her, she gives away," her uncle said with a sad laugh. "You think it's easy selling watches? I run around all the time like a chicken that's lost its head. You look at my office. I keep a stack of business cards — some good, some bad. And I drive all over the place. People say no, I come back. Sometimes they throw me out of their store, they are so sick of this face!" Her uncle sniffed, touching the side of his nose with his thumb. "It's not easy. I used to sell briefcases, but everyone has a laptop now. Who needs briefcases?"

"It isn't easy," June said. She felt bad for her uncle. Ever since she could remember, she had felt sorry for him. He always seemed to be struggling. Of her father's five siblings, he was the youngest and, unlike her father, who got his Ph.D. in the United States, her uncle had been a mediocre student in Taiwan and now made a precarious living as a salesman. June's mother liked to emphasize how poor his family was. Before June flew out to Los Angeles, her mother said she would be giving Gerard five hundred dollars for his high school graduation, and she reminded June to pick up the check when her uncle took her out for dinner.

Of course, her uncle wasn't truly *poor*. When her grandfather died, his children inherited equal portions of his land in Taiwan, and her uncle sold his share and used the money to buy the house he now lived in. No doubt things were still tight for him. When June's older sister got married two years ago, his family could not afford the extra expense of attending the wedding, and her uncle sent the bride and groom a pair of fake Rolex watches that fogged up in humid weather.

It must have been an unusual extravagance on her uncle's part when his family flew all the way out to the East Coast to visit hers ten years ago. June remembered she went to bed before her uncle's family arrived late at night, and in the morning she found her cousin asleep downstairs on the red flowery couch, June's large gray cat curled beside her. It was snowing outside, and the scene reminded June of a picture in a magazine. Helen's face was dreamy and remote as the snow fell lightly through the windows. The cat gazed at June, his mouth curved as if he were smiling.

Helen opened her eyes and sat up on the couch, blinking. "I've never seen snow before," she said when she looked out the window.

June laughed. "You haven't?"

"It doesn't snow in California. Is this your cat?" Helen tried to stroke his head, but the cat jumped off the couch and walked beneath a table, where he couldn't be touched.

"He'll love you more if you ignore him," June said.

Helen didn't listen to June's advice. The cat was banished to the basement when Helen's parents found out—they thought the cat was dirty and might trigger one of Gerard's asthma attacks—but for the rest of the trip, whenever Helen could, she snuck down to the basement and tried to lure the cat from its hiding place. The cat was not afraid of her, only disinterested. He often perched on top of the vertical end of a mattress that leaned against the wall, and Helen would entreat him to come down, repeating his name and clicking her tongue as he stared at her with supercilious calm. The only thing that tempted him was a can of treats that she would shake, and then the cat would yawn and approach her dutifully, lifting each piece from her hand with a delicate tongue, careful not to bite her.

Her uncle's family returned to Los Angeles, and two weeks later June received in the mail a softly colored ink portrait of her cat that Helen must have drawn from memory.

Dear June,

I miss Manny very much. I hope you like this picture I did of him. I'm sorry he had to live in the basement when we stayed at your house. He must be happier now that he can go upstairs.

Love,
Helen

Beneath the tip of Helen's pen, June's smug cat had undergone a transformation. She had drawn only his face and given him fine long hairs, a flesh pink nose, and warm gold eyes. His expression was sad and benevolent, as if the cat had once been human. June liked the picture very much but neglected to write and thank Helen when she returned to college.

"You talk to Helen, okay?" Her uncle caught the wheel and turned sharply into a subdivision of Spanish-style houses with red-tiled roofs. "Tell her to study. To work hard," he said as they pulled into the driveway of his home. "You be a good influence on her, I know it."

Helen and Gerard came downstairs to offer their greetings. Helen's long hair was pulled back into a ponytail, and she was taller than June expected, very slender still, with light brown skin. She spoke in a quiet, whimsical way and apologized for her mother, who was tired and had already gone to sleep.

"What do you think of this house?" her uncle asked.

"It's very nice," June said, looking around.

"Not as nice as your parents' house, right? Your parents' house much bigger than this?"

"It's not much bigger."

"We clean a lot," Helen mused, "but the house never looks clean."

"Oh, it's fine," June said. "You have a very nice house." She wasn't exactly lying. Given the fuss that was always made over how much her uncle struggled, the house itself, with its stucco walls and cathedral ceiling, was much grander than she had expected. But the house was just like her uncle's van, a good, respectable structure ruined by the clutter inside. Someone in the family was an incurable pack rat and could not bear to throw anything away. An old computer sat on top of stacked chairs in the front hall, extra tables jutted out in front of doorways, and every flat surface—countertop, table, mantel, shelf—was crowded with papers, boxes, and unending bric-a-brac. June glimpsed ceramic figurines, a brass swan, teacups, dusty bottles of whiskey and cognac, vases stuffed with artificial flowers, and jars filled with sesame candy, coins, and seashells. Things too were in the most unlikely places. Lamps stood on cookie tins in the living room, her uncle's shirts hung from the handlebars of a treadmill, a mattress set rested against the dining room table, paper towels were stored inside the fireplace, and books had been inserted between the balusters of the stairway.

They gave her a can of Coke and invited her to watch television with them. June sank down onto a battered couch that had lost its cushions. She could feel a bar and springs beneath her. Helen joined her on the couch, her uncle watched from the kitchen table, and Gerard continued to hover awkwardly in the middle of the family room. Once a skinny boy, he had become tall and stout, and his thick arms dangled softly at his sides. He didn't seem to know what to do with himself and put one hand in his pants pocket.

"Gerard, aren't you going to sit?" June asked.

Gerard smiled, his lips pressed close together. It was a smirk, but he also seemed genuinely embarrassed.

"He has a poor back," Helen said.

Her uncle perked up at this, and he began telling June the whole story. A year ago, Gerard began to have back pain and their doctor told him he had a herniated disk from all those hours of sitting in a bad chair in front of his computer. "He sat like this," her uncle said, tipping forward in his chair.

"Oh, that isn't good," June said.

"Or he sat like this." Her uncle crossed one leg beneath him and pretended to type furiously in midair. "You have to sit with both feet on the ground, you see, Gerard?"

"Okay," Gerard said with a note of annoyance.

"We bought him an expensive chair." Her uncle pointed to an empty box in the middle of the room with a shiny black office chair pictured on it. "The doctor said he should do exercises for his back. And he should pick up things like this." Her uncle squatted on the floor and demonstrated how to lift a heavy object.

"Have you been feeling better, Gerard?"

Gerard smiled at June with twisted lips. "Not really."

"He likes to stand now instead of sit," Helen said.

"Only seventeen years old!" her uncle sighed.

At midnight, her uncle dragged the mattress and box spring out of the dining room and stacked them on the living room floor. "Don't worry, I clean it for you," he said, and he proceeded to wipe down the entire set with a damp towel.

"That's okay," June said, but it was impossible to stop him. He reminded her of her father, who could be obsessive about cleaning and often woke everyone up with his vacuuming. June waited for the mattress to dry before putting on the sheets, and then Helen and Gerard wished her good night and went upstairs to bed.

From where she lay, June could see the dim light of the kitchen and hear a clock ticking somewhere in the foyer. Her uncle was still awake, eating a midnight snack and listening to a Mandarin pop song on the radio.

Helen didn't seem to have changed much from the ten-year-old girl June had known. She was still serious and shy, and she gave June an impression of thoughtful sincerity. If anything surprised June, it was how calm and centered she seemed.

The biggest change had occurred in Gerard, not Helen.

June remembered he had been a hyper, crazy kid. In all the group photographs of their two families, there was always an adult hand pressing down on Gerard's shoulder, an almost rabid gleam in his eyes as he crouched, ready to spring away. June and her sister had taken their younger cousins and brother to the Baltimore Aquarium one day, and when they went to the cafeteria for lunch, Gerard loaded as much food as possible onto his tray—pizza and fried chicken, a hamburger with French fries, a grilled cheese sandwich, a chocolate doughnut. Everyone except Helen had laughed at him, and June made him return most of the food, but Gerard didn't understand why what he'd done seemed so funny to them.

Soon after her cousins returned to Los Angeles, June found a photograph of herself holding her cat that had been left out on her desk. Someone had drawn pointed fangs on the cat, and June herself had been given blue pimples and two horns sticking out of her head. A caption scrawled below read "THE FAT GANG." Her brother laughed out loud when she showed it to him, but he said he wasn't responsible. "It must have been Gerard," he told her. June felt rather vexed by Gerard's prank. She had always been sensitive about her weight. She wasn't fat for an American, just fat for a Chinese. So now the American diet had wreaked its havoc on Gerard as well . . .

She dozed off and woke up again in the middle of the night to find the kitchen light turned off and her uncle at the top of the stairs shaking something out. It looked as if he were straightening a pillowcase, or maybe he was exercising, she couldn't tell in the darkness, but his movements were as frantic as ever, and she wondered if he would ever go to bed.

In the morning, when she opened her eyes, she found herself staring at a large oil painting on the wall of a lurid, industrial Venice. The domed buildings were infernally lit, lapped by dank green water, and a small pudgy man gazed up at a tiny, ineffectual moon. June couldn't help but smile. Her parents had bought similar stuff at a sidewalk art sale, and she had upset them one day when she took all their ugly paintings down and hid them in the basement.

On her way upstairs to take a shower, June passed by the kitchen and said hello to her aunt, who looked up from the batter she was mixing and gave her a slight smile. Her gray sweater vest looked oddly familiar to June, and it was a bit of shock when she realized that the vest was something her sister had worn in high school. Her uncle had over the years called up her father to ask for their old, spare clothes, and June's family had gone through their closets, weeding out all the things that no longer fit or were out of fashion and then sending these in a box to Los Angeles.

Gerard came out of the bathroom, and June noticed he had not flushed the toilet. She couldn't stop herself and said in a light, bantering voice, "Gerard, can't you flush?"

"What?" her uncle said, appearing around the corner. "He didn't flush the toilet? What kind of person are you, Gerard?"

"Sorry," Gerard muttered.

For breakfast, they ate a fruitcake her aunt had made by substituting olive oil for butter because Gerard was on a diet. The doctor had said he needed to lose twenty pounds and also that his cholesterol was too high.

Helen asked June how long she was going to stay with them, and June replied she was leaving early the next morning. Everyone was shocked by this news, and her uncle especially seemed disappointed. "I thought you will be here the entire week," he said.

"I'm meeting a friend in San Diego," June said. "Didn't my father tell you?"

"Why you get your father to call me?" her uncle said. "Don't you know you can call me yourself?"

"I thought it would be easier if my dad called you," June

said, feeling embarrassed. She had to admit that it didn't make much sense asking her father to be the intermediary, but whenever she spoke to his side of the family she felt they didn't understand exactly what she was saying. Even with her father, she often had to raise her voice and repeat herself to get her meaning across. But the fact that her father was unable to communicate clearly to his own brother about the length of her stay made June suspect the problem wasn't a language barrier at all — that her father and uncle and their entire side of the family just didn't pay attention, slightly deaf to the world and to each other.

Her uncle now revealed to them his plan for the day. He had to make his rounds and could drop them off where they liked and then pick them up in a few hours.

"You have to work on Saturdays?" June asked.

"How do you think I make any money?" her uncle said, rubbing his thumb and forefinger together. "Every day I have to try."

"What do you want to do?" Helen asked June.

"Let's go to the beach. It's gorgeous outside."

Gerard let out a whining hum.

"What's wrong, Gerard?" June asked.

"I don't want to go."

"Why not? Don't you ever go to the beach?"

"No."

"Why not?"

Gerard paused. "I have sensitive skin."

"He's afraid of sunburn," Helen said.

"But I'm paler than you," June said, putting her arm next to his. "We won't go for too long. And you can put sunblock on."

Helen and Gerard went upstairs to get ready, and her uncle

took June aside. "You talk to Helen, okay?" he said, and June
nodded.

It was low tide at the beach, and people were climbing over
rocks to look at the shallow pools that had formed. June sat on
the sand with her cousins and took the sunblock out of her bag,
passing it over to Gerard, who did nothing but stare at it.
"Don't you want to put some on?" she asked. "I thought you
were afraid of getting burnt."

"Here, Gerard," Helen said, and she took the tube from
him and squeezed a dollop onto each of his arms. Gerard began
to spread it slowly in a straight line with one finger, and June
felt exasperated just watching him. He was like a child and
could do nothing for himself. "You have to rub it over your
entire arm," she told him. Helen helped Gerard spread the lo-
tion across his arms and massage it into his skin, and when they
were done, June asked Helen if she wanted to go look at the
tide pools. They left Gerard behind, drawing patterns in the
sand with a stick he had picked up.

June wasn't wearing sturdy shoes, and she tread carefully
over the slippery rocks, listening to the crunch of barnacles
beneath. Helen was a few feet ahead, bent over one of the small
pools left from the receding tide. When June caught up with
her, she saw Helen holding a purple starfish in her hand. One
of its arms had broken off.

"Is it alive?" Helen asked. "I won't take it home if it's
alive."

The starfish didn't move at all when June held it. There
were traces of a jellylike substance along its arms where it had
clung to a rock. June thought it should be less brittle if it were

alive, that it should give way some, but she wasn't sure. "Shouldn't it be able to regenerate the missing arm?" she said.

An older woman wearing a yellow T-shirt paused to look at the starfish they were holding. "Do you think it's alive?" Helen asked her.

"Alive or dead," the woman said, "you don't want to take that thing back with you. Starfish have a really bad smell out of the water."

Helen reluctantly put the starfish back into the tide pool. She looked chastened, though June knew she wanted to take the starfish home. They followed the woman over the rocks and located a cluster of starfish — whole starfish — brilliant and still, along the underside of a rock. One of them was bright orange, the color of a tiger lily.

A seagull hopped and fluttered along the shore, dragging Helen's starfish in its beak. It did a little dance in the air, as if it were trying to lift itself up, but the starfish slipped from its beak and fell into the water. The seagull flapped down to retrieve it.

"Seagulls eat starfish?" Helen asked.

They watched the seagull snap up the starfish, trying several times to get a proper hold. It eyed June and Helen for a moment before spreading its wings, flying only a short distance before it dropped the starfish again. The starfish fell from a spectacular height, bouncing off a rock. Immediately a large wave came in, flooding it over.

"We should go back," June said, worried that the tide was coming in. Helen nodded, and they climbed back over the rocks. From a distance, they could see Gerard standing and poking at something with his stick.

"Does Gerard have any friends?" June asked.

Helen hesitated. "Not really."

"It just seems like he can't do anything by himself. Why is that?"

Helen shrugged. "I guess he's used to us doing everything for him. My mom still cuts his toenails."

"What?" June laughed.

Helen smiled. "We must seem odd to you."

June thought about her own family, and said, "Not that odd."

"I feel bad for him," Helen said. "My parents are always worrying about him. He's not sure of himself, I think. At least my parents gave me a little more space. I was expected to help out and do things."

"Are you two close?"

Helen reflected for a moment. "Maybe when we were younger. I remember he used to wear this jacket of mine that he loved. But the kids at school made fun of him for wearing a girl's jacket, so he stopped."

As the three of them walked back into town, June studied Gerard with curiosity. His parents' love had made him soft, dull, and useless, yet he would always be dear to them no matter what. Such love was a curse and a blessing. For who else in the world would ever love Gerard so blindly?

"Gerard," June said. "Tell me something about yourself."

He shrugged, half smiling.

"What is it that you really want?" she asked him. "What do you like doing?"

"I don't know. I like to be on my computer, I guess."

"You're just like my brother. You like to play games, right?"

"Yeah."

"What is it about the games you like?"

He gave her a shy smile, looking embarrassed. "It's fun, I guess." She felt him shrinking under her gaze, his lips pressed close together and his hands in his pockets. This inquisition of hers was evidently causing him pain, and she stopped herself.

They had agreed to meet her uncle in front of a large discount store. The window displayed child mannequins with pale brittle hair and glass blue eyes that held a sad clairvoyance. The tan of the children's skin had flaked off to reveal a whiteness underneath, and their curved arms floated awkwardly in front of them, their heads tilted sideways in wonder.

As June and her cousins were early, they wandered inside the store and ended up in the pet department. There were no cats or dogs to look at, just a few tanks of fish and some hamsters in a cage. June wanted to leave, but Helen had stopped in front of a display of bettas sitting in little plastic cups lined on a shelf. She stared at the fish for a long time, and June wondered whether she wanted to buy one. The fish were iridescent though faded, like wilted peacock feathers, each one breathing heavily at the bottom of its cup.

A salesman approached, and Helen asked how long the fish could live in the plastic cups.

"Oh, a long time," the salesman said. "In the wild, they live in tiny pockets of water just like these cups."

Helen hesitated. "It just seems like they're unhappy."

The salesman held up a mirror to one of the fish, and immediately its gills flowered. "You see that?" he said. "You put two of them together, and they'll end up killing each other. They're Siamese fighting fish." He grabbed a plastic bag from the workstation and filled it with a little water from a nearby tank. "I kid you not," he said, twisting the bag shut, leaving only a mouthful of air, "these fish come to us shipped just like this." Helen nodded when he looked at her. "I know it seems cruel, but these fish can live in just a little bit of water. I dropped a fish wrapped up like this behind a tank once. I found him three months later, and you know what, that fish was still alive. I kept the fish myself because I could hardly believe it. He lived another two years under my care. I kid you not, these fish are hardy creatures."

Helen looked at the bettas languishing in their plastic cups, and June asked if she wanted one.

"I don't have enough money," Helen said.

"That's okay, I'll buy it," June said. "It will be a gift."

"Helen," Gerard muttered beneath his breath, "Mom and Dad won't like it."

"All right then," the salesman said. "You just have to pick the one that you want."

Helen couldn't decide and kept comparing one fish to another. She finally chose one with red fins whose body had turned gray from sitting in its cup for so long.

"He's a pretty one," the salesman said, winking at her.

Along with the fish, June purchased for Helen a glass bowl, a can of fish flakes, and a bag of crystal rocks. They sat on some steps outside and waited for June's uncle. Helen balanced the plastic bag containing the fish carefully on her lap. The fish was sealed in its own little bubble, and Helen touched the bag lightly with her fingertips as though she were afraid it might burst. "I wonder if he's all right. Do you think he'll live?" she asked, studying the fish as it drifted at the bottom of the bag.

"He'll be okay."

Helen smiled and thanked June for the gift. "Do you know I've never had a pet before?"

"You haven't?" June said.

"No, my parents wouldn't let me. They thought animals were dirty and told me I had allergies."

"Not even a fish?"

Helen shook her head. "It was hard enough for them to let me have stuffed animals. They thought there was a lot of dirt and dust trapped inside the fur. At night, before I went to sleep, they would give me a stuffed animal, but it would be wrapped inside a plastic bag. Or they would put the stuffed animal inside a box and tell me I couldn't open it. I really wanted to have a pet, though. Something I could take care of."

When June's uncle picked them up, he asked Helen what she was holding as she got into the back seat.

"A fish," she replied.

"I bought it for her as a present," June said.

"What do you want to do with a fish? Eat him?" her uncle joked. Helen was silent. "Why you buy a fish? All a fish does is eat and go to the bathroom. What's the point? It's a waste of money."

"Uncle, he really wasn't expensive," June said. "Besides, he's pretty to look at."

"That fish? It's going to die any minute. I'm going to flush him down the toilet when we get home."

June hoped her uncle was kidding. He seemed truly annoyed about the fish, and they rode the rest of the way back in silence. When they were close to home, Helen leaned forward in her seat and looked earnestly at her father. "When I was little, why did you put my stuffed animals in a plastic bag? Didn't you realize I thought they were suffocating? Why would you do something like that?"

"I don't know what you're talking about," he muttered. "What is she talking about?" he asked, looking at June.

At home, Helen rinsed the rocks and treated the water as

the salesman had instructed her to do. Then she untied the bag and poured the fish into the bowl. She and June watched the betta, its first stunned reaction to being immersed in another world, and then its recollection of itself as it wriggled through the water. In just a few minutes, its color changed, and June was struck by the vivid red flame curving in the water. The fish swam in its own glass world, rising and falling, trapped in a monastic dream of blue and clear stones.

They went out to a Chinese seafood restaurant that night. June's aunt pulled disposable chopsticks out of her purse for them to use, as well as plastic straws, so that none of them would have to place their lips against their glasses of water.

"This is really expensive," Gerard said beneath his breath as he studied the menu.

"It's okay," her uncle said. "June's here, and we want to give her a nice dinner."

"Mom's food tastes better."

"Don't worry so much, Gerard," June said. Her aunt glanced over at her, and June realized she had misspoken. Her aunt had never warmed to her and no doubt thought her untrustworthy, glib, and overly Americanized—all of which was true. She must have noticed June staring at her sweater vest earlier that day because she had changed into a striped gray blouse with a low, frilled collar. With her tight poodle perm, her aunt was more somber and confident, less flashy and naïve, than when she had married June's uncle and come to live with him in New Jersey. The first time the newlyweds visited June's family, her aunt had worn a flimsy polka-dotted dress, her lipstick a shade too bright and her frizzy mass of hair pinned back with a plain brown barrette. June's mother later observed that this new wife was a sloppy dresser—had they seen her slip hanging from the bottom of her dress? At night, her aunt had worn large, thick glasses that made her look even younger, more forlorn. She spoke little and stayed in her room whenever she could, keeping her distance from them all. Perhaps she sensed the entire family judging her.

The waitress came to their table, and her uncle asked about the flounder. "Is it fresh?" he said in Chinese.

The waitress pointed to the large fish tanks lining the wall. "They're alive, aren't they? How much more fresh do you want?"

"How about the steamed dish here? It's better than the fried?"

"How do I know what you like?"

"Well, is it any good?"

"Good or bad, it's up to you to decide."

Her uncle rubbed his chin as he studied the menu. "Maybe we won't order the fish," he muttered.

"There's a mosquito on the wall," Gerard observed.

"Where?" her uncle asked, looking anxiously around him.

"There." Gerard pointed, and her uncle got up from his chair and slammed the menu against it.

After her uncle had ordered, he looked over at his daughter, then said to June, "You need to help Helen find a boyfriend, okay?"

"Oh!" Helen said, looking away and shading her eyes with her palm.

"Helen doesn't need my help," June said. "What about me? I don't have a boyfriend."

"Why not?" her uncle asked.

"Too picky," her aunt said with a faint smile.

"When are you going to get married?" her uncle demanded. "We are *wai*-ting!"

June was relieved when the dishes began to arrive. Helen asked about her trip to San Diego, and June told her she was going to rent a car tomorrow and drive down to pick up a friend, and then the two of them would drive along the coast to Mexico.

"Mexico!" her uncle said dubiously. June was afraid he would begin telling her it was too dangerous and that she was out of her mind, something she had already heard from her parents, but instead he said, "Lucky you! You get to see the world! That has always been my *mengxiang*."

Meng meant "dream," and *xiang* meant "to think." So her uncle had said traveling had been his "dream thought"?

"But you can always go to Mexico!" she said. "It's less than two hours from here."

"Yes," her uncle said with a sigh. "But see, I have almost no hair left?"

"But my dad is older than you, and he doesn't feel that way."

"Your dad is fat and rich. Of course he lives a long time. But see?" Her uncle leaned back and tightened his belt a notch. His wife looked over at him, saying nothing and chewing slowly.

When the waitress came with their check, June, who had been waiting for this moment, snatched up the bill tray and said she would be treating. Her uncle asked her to give him the check and she said no. "Let me just look over it to see if they charged the right amount," he said. June shook her head. She got her credit card out and waved to get the waitress's attention. It was then that her uncle took action. He stood up and went over to where June was sitting and seized the tray, pressing her thumb so hard that she let out a little cry of pain. He handed June's credit card back to her and returned to his seat with an air of grim triumph. "You want to treat your uncle," he muttered, "but how can I let you do that?"

The waitress came and took the check from him, and her uncle said to June, "Next time you want to visit, all you do is pick up the phone and say, 'Uncle, this is June. I'm coming down this weekend.' Okay? You live close by and should visit more. Don't avoid us because Gerard can't flush the toilet."

"This is your fault!" her aunt said, slapping the table with a flat hand. "You confuse him! You tell him to save water and not to flush."

"I tell him that?" her uncle said, looking bemused.

On their way home, they stopped at a video store to rent a movie. June and her cousins watched it together in the family room, she and Helen perched on the broken couch, Gerard standing nearby, shifting from one foot to the other. Only when the movie was over did June realize that she had forgotten to speak to Helen about the Christian cult she was involved in. There was no delicate way of approaching the subject, and it seemed awkward to do so now when everyone was tired and getting ready to go to bed.

She wasn't truly worried about Helen, who struck her as the sanest member of that household. It was only a shame that Helen, burdened by such a neurotic family, should try to slip free by submitting to another form of control. She reminded June of a character in a Chekhov story, sensitive and kind, with a soul "as soft as wax." She could do much with her life if only she were given the right circumstances.

In the middle of the night, June awoke to hear the front door unlocking and saw Helen standing in the foyer, her long hair shadowing her face, a light jacket over her nightgown. "Where are you going?" June asked her.

"I can't sleep," Helen said. "I want to walk around."

"Wait, I'll go with you." June got up and slipped on her shoes, quietly following Helen to the coolness outside and shutting the door behind her.

They walked in a loop around Helen's neighborhood, and June liked the dark rows of silent houses, how odd it felt to be passing by them at night when everyone else was sleeping. Sometimes, a light still burned in one of the windows. Or they saw a distant light shining through the pines. They continued walking, their chests expanding in the darkness, passing houses that seemed to possess a photographic stillness, to be on the verge of a memory or a dream.

"Your father wanted me to talk to you about your church," June said.

Helen gave her a quick glance. "He told you about all that?"

June nodded. "I hope that's okay."

"I'm just embarrassed."

"Your dad is really worried. He's afraid you're going to lose your scholarship."

"I know," Helen said. "Ever since my parents found out, they've been forcing me to come home every weekend. I was hoping my church would sponsor me for a trip to China this summer, but my parents would never let me go now."

"But why China?"

"There are people I can help there. I know it sounds silly, but I want to be a good person."

June smiled. "But you can help others and be a good person here."

"Yes," Helen said, growing quiet. Her brow was pensive

and her lips were parted slightly, a look of waiting on her face. They walked on in silence, retracing their steps and circling the neighborhood once more. "I don't know why I get depressed whenever I come home," Helen said. "It's like part of me is blunted, and I can't wait to go back and be with people who really know me, the better part of me at least. Your family always sees the worst in you, and you see the worst in them, and it's like neither of you can ever change for the better."

"That's a bleak way of looking at things," June said. "I hope that's not true." And yet she recognized what Helen was saying. It was hard not to feel limited by your family. She herself always tried to hide from them her tender spots, her weaknesses, as best she could. Why was that? There was a gap, she felt, a flaw in their understanding. Their way of looking at things, their assumptions about her and other people, so often seemed wrong, and she had learned to shy away from their judgment and even their sympathy. No doubt her brother did the same with her and the rest of the family. June could be quite callous when talking about him with her friends, saying he was a computer geek who holed himself up in his room, but what did she really know about his life? She didn't know what he did with his days, who his friends were in college, if he had ever kissed a girl or been in love. At some point, a veil had fallen between them, and now so many things were left unsaid.

"Helen," June said, reflecting a moment, "does your father ever mention his first wife?" There was a pause in which she realized she shouldn't have asked this question.

"What did you just say?" Helen asked. June was silent, and Helen said cautiously, "Was my father married before?"

June felt her mind racing as she grasped for a lie, a loophole she could slip through, but she could only nod her head. "I'm sorry. I thought you knew." She couldn't believe her own stupidity. She had never imagined her uncle would be able to keep his first marriage a secret from his family.

"Could you tell me more?" Helen asked.

"I probably shouldn't. My father is going to kill me when he finds out I told you."

"But I really want to know," Helen said. "How did you know my dad was married before?"

June hesitated. "Well, I met her," she said. "I was really young, maybe four years old, and we were visiting Taiwan. My parents asked her to babysit me and Meg for the day, and for some reason, she left a strong impression on me. I thought she was very beautiful." June remembered how this young, pretty aunt of hers had made them laugh when she bent one arm up and the other down and moved her head back and forth like an Egyptian. June and her sister had tried to imitate her in the mirror. Then they had taken a cab together to a small boutique, and there had been the prettiest sparkling things inside, and all these glittering bits had seemed to June like tokens of her aunt's beauty. She had never met anyone so lovely and was devastated when her parents returned to take her and her sister away. Her aunt smiled and bent down to kiss her—she had such bright, clear eyes!—then took the rhinestone comb out of her hair and gave it to June as a memento. During the taxi ride back to her grandmother's apartment, June had clutched the comb in her hand and felt a delirious happiness. She put the charmed comb in her hair, fully expecting something wonderful to happen, but when she had a chance to look at herself in the mirror, it did not look so nice—or maybe it was *she* who did not look so nice. The comb was too large and slipped from her hair. She took it out to inspect it more carefully and noticed for the first time that one of the little rhinestones was missing.

Soon after his divorce, her uncle drove down from New Jersey and stayed with them one weekend. He ended up moping about in his room, staring at recent photographs of his ex-wife which he had dumped in a pile on the bed. He picked up one photo after another, passing it over for June to look at, and she could hardly recognize the lovely aunt she remembered. Her aunt looked tired and plain, without any makeup on. She did not smile in any of the photographs.

"She's completely changed, right?" her uncle said.

"She looks sad."

"Yes," he said. "But why is she so sad? Why not smile at the camera? Why so sad?"

"She gave me a comb from her hair," June said. "I liked her."

Her uncle sighed. "People change. She's not pretty anymore."

Her uncle married again a year later, and his second wife seemed nothing like the first. It was impossible for June not to compare them, and perhaps the story she told her cousin implied this because Helen turned to look at her, and said, "My mom was beautiful, too, when she was young."

"Yes," June said.

"Do you know why his first marriage ended?"

"I think your dad left her alone in Taiwan for the first year he was starting out in the U.S. He asked his cousin to look after her while he was away. When your dad came back to visit, she was cold to him and claimed she'd been raped by a cabdriver. No one knew if this story was true or not. Your dad went back to New Jersey, and in two weeks he received a letter from his wife saying she wanted a divorce. She was in love with his cousin. The two had been having an affair for all this time, and now they wanted to get married. The news was quite a blow to your dad. He and his cousin had grown up together, and your dad considered him his best friend."

"I feel so sorry for him."

"I know."

"It's just so strange to think all this happened to him," Helen said. "I would never have guessed it was possible. Your parents always seem so . . . devoid of mystery, you know what I mean?"

June smiled. "Did you ever look through the old family albums in Grandma's apartment? Maybe everyone looks better in black and white, or maybe it's just that everyone seems more beautiful because they're young. But your dad was really handsome then." She had once expressed surprise to her mother about her uncle's striking looks, and her mother had said he was photogenic but that all his beauty evaporated the instant he opened his mouth. In the photographs, he had a dark, intense gaze that was mysterious and appealing, but in person her uncle's stare revealed an obsessive anxiety, an inward spiraling of some kind. He had been born with a birthmark staining his face which ran slantwise from the corner of his mouth all the way down to his chin. Children had teased him in school and called him Black Mouth, and her uncle had been self-conscious about the mark and finally gotten it removed by a surgeon when he came to the United States.

"I'm glad you told me," Helen said. "I feel like maybe I can understand him a little more." They had returned to the house, and she wished June good night.

.　　.　　.

June was surprised when both her cousins woke up early the next morning to see her off. Helen looked sleepy and smiled at June, clutching her elbows as though she were cold. She seemed so thin in her nightgown . . . June wondered what would happen to her after she left. By the time they saw each other again, would Helen have seen China or would she be living with her family or would her life have taken a new, unexpected direction? She hugged Helen close and then Gerard, too. "Take care of yourselves," she said.

Gerard smiled at her with closed lips. "So," he breathed, "you're going to Mexico?" He spoke shyly from the corner of his mouth.

June nodded. "Do you want to come with me?"

He only smiled at her, one hand in his pocket.

In the car, her uncle asked June if she'd spoken to Helen.

"Uncle, I don't think you need to worry," she said. "Helen will be fine."

"You think?" her uncle said, touching the corners of his mouth. June could make out only the faintest outline of his birthmark, a slight discoloration that reminded her of a territory with fading boundaries. Her uncle stroked the spot as if he could rub it gently away. There had been a time, June remembered, when she had actively disliked her uncle. Her bad feelings toward him arose one day when, in front of her parents, her uncle squeezed her leg, and said jokingly, "Fat is sexy." She had been stunned and felt her cheeks turning red. She was only seven or eight, but she would never forget such a humiliation. Her mother said her uncle was brain-damaged and always making mistakes of this kind.

Her uncle dropped her off at a car rental place on the way to making his rounds. As she said good-bye to him, he gave her one of his watches. It had a rectangular face lined with faux diamonds and a beige leather strap. June didn't want to seem ungrateful, but she knew she would never wear it and tried to give it back to him. "I already have a watch, see?" she said, showing him the one on her wrist.

"You don't like?" her uncle said.

"It's nice. I just don't think I'll ever wear it. I don't want it to go to waste."

Her uncle hissed through his teeth as he took the watch back. He got out of the van and opened the side door, rummaging inside for a while as June stood on the sidewalk. "How about this one? You like it better?" he said, emerging from the van and handing her a small burgundy box.

A fake Cartier with a silver band was snuggled inside. June felt bad. No doubt it was more expensive than the previous watch he had given her. "You like?" he repeated.

"I do, but—"

"Cartier!" he said fiercely. "Cartier!"

"It's very nice," she said. "I like it."

"You wear this one?"

She nodded.

Her uncle smiled at her. "You have good taste. That watch is better than the other one. So you will visit us again soon, right?"

June took off her watch and put the new one on her wrist. She was surprised by how much she liked her uncle's gift—she had never liked anything he'd given her before—and she moved the dial to the center of her wrist, gazing at it for a moment before smiling up at him.

REMEDIES

Your grandmother was a funny woman, my mother says. In the afternoons, she'd get into one of those rickshaws with a bicycle attached and ask the man to take her to the movie theater. She went to see the movies every day by herself. The theater wasn't usually crowded, and you could hear the rats squeal when they got trapped in the seats. They were giant rats, as big as American house cats, and they crawled up and down the aisles, waiting for you to drop a piece of food on the floor. Everyone threw their chicken bones onto the ground, spat out litchi pits and the cracked shells of watermelon seeds, and there was always a rustling underfoot as people shifted in their seats and the rats glided between their legs.

Your grandma really liked the movies. There was one movie in particular. A famous Chinese actress drowns herself in the Hangzhou lake. The day after she saw it, your grandma took a bus to the suburbs outside Taipei and jumped into the river. The water was too shallow, and she twisted her ankle on the rocks. A local fisherman picked her out of the water, all dripping and torn. She had worn bright yellow silk for the occasion.

You have to understand that your grandma tried to cure herself many times. She would hear of some new remedy and be convinced this would make her well again. For a while, she visited the local hospital, collecting placentas. She cooked a soup with the bags because she thought the hormones would make her strong again. She also kept a container of crawling insects, not too large, like shiny beetles. She fed the insects a high-quality medicine—it was ground into a powder and smelled very sweet—and she would eat one of these insects live each morning. She did this for six months. But she did not get any better.

Bad things can happen to you when you take leave of the dead. That's what my uncle, the feng shui expert, says. He sits at his dining room table, poking a snail out of its shell with a toothpick. In front of us are a mound of steaming shells, brown-and-white-checkered, the kind that my hermit crabs used to live in. The snail comes out with a sound of suction. My uncle pops it into his mouth and then with one hand waves at the plate in front of us. "Eat, eat!" he says as he chews. My father has already taken a heaping spoonful, my mother a lesser portion, and when the dish comes around to me I let two or three shells clink onto my plate. There was a time, I think, when I ate snails and liked them. This was before language, when all things were equal and strange. I remember the salty taste of their shells, the curled, rubbery meat against my tongue.

My uncle is not really my uncle, but that's what I call him. He is distantly related to my father, and they play golf together on the weekends. He used to be the manager of a bank, but then he quit his job to study feng shui. For a couple hundred dollars, he will go to your home or your office and tell you if the setting is propitious. He will ask for the date and hour of your birth and determine how the location will affect your destiny. Each place has a different impact on each person, he says. A pond or a fountain will be a good influence on someone with wood in them, but it will spell disaster for a person with too much fire. It is a delicate task. There are important distinctions to be made, and these will affect a lifetime. "I am a powerful man," my uncle says, "but it is a burden. I do not ever give my advice lightly."

Now my uncle tells us a story of his father, who almost died when he visited his aunt on her deathbed. This aunt was a widow with no children, and when the last breath left her body, her eyes fell directly upon him. My uncle's father bowed before her three times and felt immediately as if he had swallowed something cold. He collapsed onto the floor and couldn't move. The family called in a fortune-teller, who told them that his illness was the result of a bad interaction with his aunt's spirit. The fortune-teller recommended that the aunt be cremated, her ashes buried as soon as possible, and when this was done, my uncle's father awoke from his sickness.

"You have to be very careful when you take leave of the dead," my uncle says. "Better not to show too much grief. Do not bow before the dead, because it opens you up to their influence."

I look at my mother and wonder if she is thinking the same thing. She once showed me a picture of my grandmother when she was a young woman. I couldn't believe it. "It's like she's another person," I said. Her cheeks were smooth and round, her lips parted slightly to reveal a glimmer of a tooth. Her mouth had not yet caved in, and she had not formed the habit of lifting her bottom lip to close the gap. I looked at her small, bright eyes, and when I tilted my head I had a strange feeling of looking at myself. It was the first time I ever saw my face rising beneath the surface of hers.

Your grandfather thought her illness was psychological, my mother said. The last time he saw her in good health was when she boarded a train to Wuxi to take care of her mother. Her mother died, and two months later your grandfather went to the station to pick her up. He could not recognize her when she got off the train. She was completely changed. She had lost more than forty pounds, and she could no longer keep food in her.

It is difficult for me to imagine my grandmother having a life apart from her illness. Ever since I knew her, she had been steeped in sickness, her body emanating an odor of mothballs and the bitter herbs that she drank with her tea. Her face was gaunt and androgynous, thinly bordered by soot gray hair, and her mouth often moved in a circular motion as if she were chewing. In her later years, she suffered a stroke, and her right hand became a useless claw that she kept near her stomach. When she tried to speak to my mother, I heard her false teeth shifting around in her mouth as she shaped the words with a thick, rounded tongue.

Sometimes, when we were outside, I held her by the arm as she walked so she wouldn't topple over. In winter, she wore a ratty coat of dark synthetic fur. At eight years old, I stood at her shoulder, and when she leaned against me I felt how light and frail she was. I loved her as easily as I loved a doll that is broken, but I never liked how she smelled, sometimes of herbs and sometimes of baby powder, as if she were trying to cover her sickness. Her tiny eyes pierced me with their secret life. She had been a math teacher in Nanjing, my mother said. Her gnarled left hand tightened around my wrist with a pressure stronger than words.

When dinner is over, my uncle goes over to his desk and brings out three slivers of rice paper, each one about the size of a bookmark. "You have all been so good to me," he says. "I wanted to give you a gift in return." On each slip of paper, my uncle has written characters in red ink. At the bottom, there are two lines of inverted *V*'s that look like teepees or a child's representation of flying birds. "If you believe in this," my uncle says, "keep it with you at all times. One day, when you find yourself in real trouble, you should burn this paper, mixing the ashes in a cup of water. Drink half the cup and pour what is left into your bath. If you believe in this paper, it will protect you. If you don't believe, burn it, for it will harm you."

I look down at my yellow slip of paper. There is already a smudge on two of the characters. Could it be a drop of my uncle's saliva, my own sweat, the water from the edge of my glass? My parents, I know, will hold on to their slips of paper. My mother already believes in it, I can tell by the way she folds it carefully into her wallet. My father will keep it out of sheer indifference. Like a true skeptic, he will forget about it entirely by the time he goes home to bed tonight.

As for myself, I don't want to think too much about it. My uncle is a charismatic, wily man who knows how to play on a person's fears. If you don't believe, burn it, he says. Yet if I burned it, it would be because I was afraid of what it might do. If I burned it, it would mean that I really believed in its power.

I don't believe in it. Not really.

Yet I examine it more closely, drawn to it because it holds both a curse and a promise.

GIVING A CLOCK

Sometimes I get a glimpse of what my aunt used to be. Like now, as she snores like a horse at the back of the car. She was once a sturdy woman. She would talk to me with a slippered foot hanging off the kitchen table. Walking home afterward, I saw my father's mouth crease at a funny angle. Your aunt is truly something. Showing us her underwear! And it wasn't that she was immodest. She was earthy and obtuse. She was all skin that I couldn't avoid. When I was a child, I was scared of her painted eyebrows. They were darker than the rest of her face, arching to an ominous point. She would come into our house, blowing smoke in the air, and the smell would soak into my hair like perfume.

My mother was not like this. At four years old, I couldn't describe the difference except by telling her one day in the kitchen that I thought she was prettier. Don't tell Auntie, I said. But my mother betrayed me that very evening, speaking in Chinese because she thought I wouldn't understand. All the grown-ups burst out laughing, and then my aunt turned to

74

look at me. "So you think I'm not as pretty?" she said. My fingers trailed along the sofa as I moved away from her. "You think your mom is prettier than me, hey?" All at once, she lunged, squeezing me tight. When she suctioned my face with kisses, I could feel the hot steam of her emotion. She was a tyrant in that way, her passions swirled messily together, making me afraid. To love and to hate was the same, and even the dog was scared of her.

Now my aunt reminds me of a bird. Inside, a clock is ticking. There is a mass of corrupted tissue wedged into her spine. It is slowly eating at the bone. She reminds me of a bird because of her delicate legs and pointed shoes. She wears a light, filmy dress, and her hair is newly permed. I have never seen her look so elegant. She smiles, moving carefully. Her body has no weight, her bones filled with air. I hold her purse. I take her arm. I have crossed over the threshold into quiet rooms without a pulse. My aunt lets out a breath, lowering herself into a chair. She rolls up her sleeve without seeming to bend her fingers. When she presents her arm to the nurse, it is as if she is giving away her life. The nurse holds her wrist, and my aunt closes her eyes. Something is dripping into her veins. It is a long, leisurely infusion. The nurse touches her arm, and my aunt opens her eyes again. When she looks at me, it's as if I'm not there. "This disease is playing tricks on me," she says.

My mother and aunt have sharp tongues inherited from my grandmother. My mother is cool and sardonic, her method precise. Her words slice my heart into fine strips. Take an antidepressant, she says when I tell her I am lonely and want to come home. My aunt, on the other hand, knows nothing whatever about slipping needles under a person's skin. Her violence is sudden and elemental and creates its own atmosphere. In their circle of friends, both sisters are known to keep their husbands in line.

There is nothing simple about the life that flourishes in my aunt's house. Plants struggle into existence with broken spines. The pots are too small, and the sun staggers in through long vertical windows. My aunt will forget to water her plants for weeks at a time, and as they sit and burn in the sun, parts of themselves curl, darken, and fall off. Then my aunt will give them a little water to drink. Somehow the plants thrive, each year assuming more stubborn, fantastical shapes. I sense their breathing—all that complex, defective life.

My aunt calls me, and I go to her bedroom. She has a separate bedroom because my uncle can't sleep with her snoring. "But that doesn't mean we don't have sex," she once told me. She lies on her side in bed in a cream negligee. Her skin is a rough brown, spotted with freckles. There is a faint, lasting smell of cigarette smoke, which seems to come from the carpet.

"For a second, I thought you were your mother," my aunt says. "She's gotten fatter, but she used to have a long, thin neck like yours. A chicken's neck, we called it."

I smile. I don't tell her that whenever my mother looks in the mirror these days, she complains about how she looks more and more like my aunt. Her face is wider and heavier, age spots spreading along her cheeks. "She's afraid of getting old and ugly like me?" my aunt would say.

My aunt gazes at me for a second. "You haven't ever been kissed, have you?" I start, and she laughs at me. "You're just like your mother, so conservative. I was worried that she would become an old maid, but then she met your father. I felt so sorry for your father, especially before they were married. Once, when they visited me, I noticed there were scratch marks on his arm. I asked where they came from, and he flushed, saying he had tried to kiss your mother in the car." My aunt chuckles. "Your mother was a real prude! You should have seen those scratches!"

She sighs and asks me for the time. "Dr. Chang is coming. He's going to make me some secret potion of his."

I ask her what is in the potion.

"Who knows? Chinese medicine that tastes bad. I'll ask him to sweeten it with rock sugar. He's most likely a fake, but I have nothing to lose."

I tell her about the acupuncturist that my friend's mother sees every week. She's supposed to be some kind of miracle worker, I say. She feels your pulse and knows what is ailing you.

"Give me her number," my aunt says. She shifts in bed, resting her face in the palm of her hand. "Do you know what I miss most of all?"

What? I ask.

"The feeling of hope. Of having a future."

Yes, I say.

"It's no good living when you have a death sentence hanging over your head."

But all of us are hoping, I say. If you only knew how much we are hoping.

"I know," she says. Her face trembles and she begins to cry. "Sometimes, it becomes such a burden — other people's hope."

I hear the sound of my cousin's motorized wheelchair as he steers himself along the hallway. He stops in front of the half-open door. The frame is too narrow for his wheelchair to pass easily through. For a moment, he stares at both of us crying, and then, without a word, continues along down the hallway.

"Why don't you take Basil out with Philip?" my aunt says. "Yes, yes," she urges. "I need to get ready for Dr. Chang."

Outside, Philip asks me if I can adjust his glasses. They are slipping down his face. I set them higher up on his nose. How's that? I say. Yes, thank you, he says. The dog barks, straining under her leash. Okay, Basil, I say, beginning to walk. Doña Basilia wishes to take a shit, Philip says.

We walk the beagle to the pond that borders the back of a neighbor's yard. Even in summer, the pond is murky brown with insects trembling on the surface. My sister and I tried to fish here when we were younger. Philip would sit a little off to the side, watching. He couldn't get too close to the water because his wheelchair would get stuck in the mud. I never caught any fish, though my sister once dragged a turtle to the edge.

I release Basil from her leash, and Philip and I watch her tear around the pond, her mouth stretched into a grin. She runs around me in circles, asking me to chase her, and when I reach for her coat, she nimbly dodges away. I look at my cousin as he stares at the pond with heavy eyelids. He is ten years older than I am, with a sensual face, unusually large and sagging. I have always wondered if his face would be the same if he could walk. The weight in his body is unevenly distributed, all in the face and stomach, while his legs grow thinner every year. Over time he has become immured within his skin. It is thick and dull, faintly tinged with blue, his blood circulating slowly in his veins. His arms and legs always feel cold, and if you pricked him with a needle, he would tell you that he felt pressure but no pain.

As a child, I was devoted to him. I cut up his food and lifted the fork to his mouth. He didn't seem to mind when I dropped pieces into his lap, staining his pants. If he wanted to blow his nose, I would fetch a tissue. His feet would fall off the footrest, and I would grab his ankles, positioning them better. Like this? I'd say. Yes, he said, thank you.

Things are not so easy between us now. He is more silent and withdrawn, and I have somehow developed *this* personality. I am more selfish, I think. There isn't the same pleasure in waiting on him as before. And he knows this.

I hook the leash onto Basil's collar and we head back to my aunt's house. Both of us laugh over the beagle's impetuous crawl. The dog strains with her nose along the ground, and I hold her back to keep myself from flying along the asphalt. My aunt watches us from the doorstep. She wears a thin robe, her arms crossed over her chest. "That dog is going to live longer than me," she says.

Philip's face stiffens. He has heard this before and is sick of his mother's talk.

"It's terrible to think that everyone will still be here when I am gone," my aunt says. "I'm afraid that all of you will go on living, you will all forget me — yes, you will forget me. Even now, all of you are living. I am the only one who is not living . . ." My cousin does not look at her as he steers himself up the ramp. When his mother makes the motions to assist him, he replies stonily that he does not need her help. But he comes to a dead stop when he gets to the door. My aunt stands in front of the door, gloating. "You don't need any help, huh?" she says.

Well, you could open the door, Philip says.

"You need my help," she replies, opening the door for him.

•   •   •

79

I sleep in the afternoon, my will folding in upon itself. When I wake up, I feel drained and without desire, wanting only sleep, as if it were some narcotic.

My mother calls me into the kitchen to eat, handing me a bowl full of noodles. She wonders if I have anemia, which she says is caused not only by poor diet but deficient kidneys. When I sit down at the table, she takes the bowl away.

It's probably not salty enough for you, she says.

She opens the refrigerator and takes out the soy sauce. You know, she says, I just want to tell you that salt causes stomach cancer. She tilts the bottle carefully and lets a drop fall onto my noodles.

I snatch the bottle away from her. I don't want to hear it, I say. I've always been vulnerable to what my mother says. No one has as much influence over me.

One day, I hope you will remember what I say, she tells me.

Please leave me alone, I tell her.

You're stubborn, just like your auntie. All those years she smoked. Always eating spicy, salty food. A terrible diet! I told her a few years ago she should have a thorough checkup. She didn't want to. Too lazy. If she had listened to me — My mother stops herself and looks at me sadly. Well, she says, I guess it's all fate. Your aunt is an unlucky person. A fortune-teller looked at her hand and told her she would live a short life.

How could someone say something like that?

This fortune-teller was blunt. Your aunt was very upset, and I told her not to worry about it. I never said anything, not even when she moved to her new house and the front door was black. Then last year, she accepted a clock for her birthday. *Song zhong.* Do you know that? It means "giving a clock" but also "going to a funeral." You don't ever give a Chinese a clock, all right? I wouldn't have taken it, but your aunt laughed. She said she wasn't superstitious.

What are you trying to do, my mother says when she sees me pouring more soy sauce onto my noodles. Are you trying to kill yourself?

In the mornings, I drive my aunt to Baltimore. It takes over an hour each way, and my aunt usually sleeps in the back of the car. I remember once during a road trip playing cards with my sister over my aunt's lap, how we smirked at each other whenever she snored. When my aunt woke up, she looked at us smiling at her. "I hope I wasn't snoring. Did I snore?"

No, I said.

She looked relieved. "You never know when you're asleep. It's so embarrassing, all the noise you make, your mouth hanging open. People tell me I snore, but I can't believe it. I don't think I'm the type of person to snore."

Yet my aunt could never hold anything in. Even buttons popped off her clothes. She would be pumping gas for her car, and her skirt would burst open at the waist and fall to the ground.

Today my aunt sits beside me because it is no use sleeping. She blinks at the sun's glare, her face and hands bloated and pale, as if she were drowned. I drive in silence, without turning on the radio. The road stretches before us like a monotonous dream. The windshield vibrates with light, burning my eyes. I forget that I am turning the wheel, my hands following the shape of the road.

"Last night, I took thirteen sleeping pills," my aunt says.

Her voice quavers, rising from inhuman depths. I'm afraid to look at her. If I look at her, I will be pulled under, unable to breathe.

"The doctor told me to take one, and if I was still awake to take another in twenty minutes. But I kept taking them. I was so miserable. My hand kept reaching out for them, and I didn't know what I was doing. I walked up and down the stairs, I sat on the floor making strange noises, I was like a monkey—a monkey!" She pauses. "It's so sad to me."

What is, Auntie? I say.

"I was thinking of your grandma. You know, she was addicted to sleeping pills. When she couldn't go to sleep, she would hit her head against the wall and cry, asking for her mother. A forty-year-old woman still asking for her mother! She didn't want any of us, even though we were living. When I was a child, I loved her more than anyone in the world. Just the thought of her dying would make me go crazy. Now I know how hopeless she felt. Every day trying to get better."

She looks at me. "I feel closest now to your mother. It's because we share the same blood, the blood of our parents mixed together. Our blood is closer to each other's than anyone else's."

I remember visiting my aunt when we first learned about her cancer, how she came down the stairs to greet us, looking only at my mother and smiling. My mother smiled as well. When they stood in front of each other, my mother took my aunt's arms, clutching her by the elbows. They stood like that for a while, holding each other by the elbows. Then my aunt rubbed my mother's back gently, and said, "With you here, I feel secure." I had brought roses for my aunt, and she seemed genuinely pleased by the sight of them. After learning her news, I had rushed out to the backyard, where our rosebushes stood, and in the dark I had cut every red, yellow, and pink bloom I could find. The roses were overblown, already dropping petals, but my aunt smiled as she gazed at them, lifting the bouquet to her nose.

But don't you feel closer to your children? I ask her.

"Not as strong," she says. "They have only half my blood. Even though they came out of my body." My aunt sighs. "I know now what my life is. My daughter is a doctor but would rather treat her patients than her sick mother. My son has no emotions and shuts himself up in his room all day and ignores me. I would have been at their side to comfort and take care of them, but they don't do that for me. I am sure they love me, but not that much. Even though they have only one mother. Only one."

At the hospital, my aunt hesitates, wandering down the wrong hallway. She walks slowly, bumping into people, an open door, the water fountain.

Mrs. Yu, the nurse says. It's this way.

My aunt ignores her, studying the physicians' names listed on the directory. When she hears a doctor talking on the phone, she moves toward him and waits expectantly. The doctor glances up at her.

Mrs. Yu, the nurse repeats as she takes my aunt's arm.

"My son is a quadriplegic," my aunt says. "The doctors said he couldn't live when he was seven, but now he's twenty-eight. We won a lawsuit a few years ago, so now he's rich, and I'm going to find a wife who he can have sex with. Isn't that wonderful?"

The nurse tells her how happy she is for him. She squeezes my aunt's hand. Now you sit right there, Mrs. Yu.

I sit beside my aunt, pretending to read a book. My aunt sighs loudly, stirring in her chair. She is waiting for me to look up. I stare mercilessly at the page, the words tunneling into my mind, then dropping away. My aunt is silent, but I feel her presence burning, insisting, without touching my skin. Her personality is submerged, or maybe it is magnified, I can't tell which. Somehow, though, she has become inseparable from her disease. She reminds me of an insect scurrying along a slippery edge, trying to keep abreast of water. I can't bear to see her frantic motions.

My aunt stands up and slowly paces to the other side of the room, her arms pressed against her stomach. She moves toward an older woman sitting quietly with folded hands. My aunt smiles at her. "What are you here for?"

Oh, the woman says, gazing at her for the first time. She did not notice my aunt creeping toward her with such fateful intention. It's not me, it's my husband.

My aunt looks at her blankly.

He's getting his radiation now, the woman says. It's near his throat.

"Me, colon cancer."

Oh, the woman murmurs.

"Yes. They took a large piece of my colon out two years ago." My aunt nods as if she is trying to understand all this herself. "They stapled me together and said I was completely cured. No need to worry, they said." My aunt nods again. "Now it's come back, growing in my spine. The size of a grape-fruit. But this time, it's inoperable, they say."

Oh, I am so sorry, the woman says.

"Yes. They don't seem to understand this is the only life you have."

No, they don't.

"That is my niece over there. She just finished her first year of college." The woman looks over at me and we both exchange a weak flutter of smiles. "She's always reading books."

Uh-huh.

"She's so good, driving me here each day."

That is nice of her, the woman says.

I wrote my aunt a few times after I returned to my university in the fall. In one letter, I told her I had always imagined we would have lunch together someday when I was older and could pick up the check. She wrote back that she liked that idea and wondered what I would be like when I was older. I remember the person I was in college. I was naïve and had a keen sense of my own importance. When I wrote her that letter, I couldn't quite believe our conversation would ever come to an end.

I looked through her old photographs not so long ago. My uncle allowed me into his library and invited me to sit down in his chair. There was an unusual softening in him. He had little patience for people of my generation and often said we were spoiled and didn't appreciate everything our parents had given us.

There was one photograph of my aunt and uncle sitting on a bench in Washington Square in New York City. My aunt's face is as round as an apple, and she is bundled up in a soft brown coat with a fur-lined collar, her shoulder resting against my uncle's. My uncle wears a dark winter coat and tie, and they look like a happy, elegant couple, sitting close beside each other, with their hands in their laps, and smiling.

You both look so young, I told my uncle.

We took a lot of pictures then, he said. Not so much later.

He picked up the photograph and gazed at it for a moment before he shook his head and put it down again. When you're young, you have the energy to take pictures, he said.

I wake up, and it is four in the morning, the windows still dark. I have just met my aunt for the first time in several years, and my mind is still tingling from her presence. I had felt such hope seeing her again.

In my dream, I am walking along a sloping field toward a group of strangers, and I see my aunt talking and laughing with a glass in her hand. She is wearing the beautiful rose dress that we buried her in. The grass glows unnaturally against the darkening sky, and I walk toward my aunt with an expanding sense of unreality, my lungs filling with cold, fragrant air. When I look down, there is the pink shimmer of her dress, which I am now wearing, her pearl necklace looped around my wrists.

The last time I spoke to my aunt, it was near Christmas. It was snowing, and the whiteness outside seemed symbolic. Everyone said that if there was a miracle, it would be today. But you don't believe in God, Philip said to me. So there can be no miracles.

My aunt was asleep from the morphine, and when she woke up she was surprised to see all of us standing around her bed. "All of you are here because I am going to die," she said. She told us that she had been dreaming of Grandpa. "We were playing mahjong together, and I was two tiles away from winning." All of us looked at my grandfather, who seemed bewildered. He didn't understand what she was saying. "I was dreaming, and I felt no pain," my aunt said to him in Chinese. "No pain. It's nice to dream like that." She closed her eyes to go back to sleep. "I don't mind dying," she said, "if death is like a dream."

If death is like a dream. I'm afraid it's a more absolute disconnection. The closest knowledge I get is when I wake up at three or four o'clock in the morning. Or maybe that time I was unconscious and they pulled out my wisdom teeth. It was a snipping of the wires, no images at all, no sensation of time passing. One moment, they were covering my mouth with a mask and I felt my body growing heavy. The next moment, a nurse was touching my arm and I realized that my mouth was full of cotton. No memory of the space in between.

But four o'clock passes. The sky begins to lighten, and I feel my blood rushing inside me.

On July Fourth, my aunt hosted a celebration on her deck. She wore a green silk Japanese robe embroidered with gold-red chrysanthemums. There was something ceremonial about her presence as she sat quietly in her chair. Her face seemed to radiate the peculiar glow of the dying. People circled and brushed clumsily against her like huge, errant moths. She smiled at them, yet remained calm and untouched. During the fireworks, everyone's gaze wandered toward her. I lit a fuse, dodged quickly away. The deck brightened, a lurid fluorescence, and I looked at all the illuminated faces. An agony of wonder. What secret things passed in the dark between us? Streaming colors, the crackle and hiss, and then darkness as everyone stared at the spent fuse. In all the pictures we took of that day, my aunt is the focal point. Her presence quietly overwhelms the others. She gazes at the camera with clear, shining eyes as if she is staring into her future.

BLUE HOUR

It was New Year's Eve, and the train to New York was crowded. Paul had been late meeting them at the station, and now he and Jeremy had rushed off to look for seats. Iris couldn't help but feel animated, as if she'd drunk a glass of wine. She wondered what the two men thought of each other. The train began to move, and she stepped quickly down the aisle. It was a feeling of anticipation, really. She sensed it in the other passengers, even though they tried not to show it, keeping their faces straight. But every time they glanced at their watches, they would be counting down the hours. Like Iris, they would be thinking of the night ahead and who they would be seeing once they got off the train.

The automatic doors of the compartment slid back, and Iris was treading on rattling metal, feeling the cold wind. Through a crack, she could see the ground hurtling beneath her feet. She felt light-headed, aware of the piece of metal on which she stood, her body separate from the rush of earth below. Then she stepped into the next car, as if entering a dark red womb, and the doors slid shut behind her, sealing off the train's roar. Bare symmetrical trees floated by along the windows.

"Iris!" Jeremy called out. He had found seats facing each other. Iris sat down beside him, even though it occurred to her that Paul might be annoyed. But she didn't want Jeremy to think that she and Paul were one of those couples whose bodies were fused together. As if they shared a leg or an organ and couldn't breathe or take a step without the other person.

The doors parted, cold air blowing in. "All tickets please!" the conductor shouted.

"When will we get there?" Paul asked as he came by.

The conductor did not look up, punching frenetic holes into their tickets. "We're like the atmosphere," he muttered. "Before you know it, we dissipate." None of them said anything, and the conductor glanced up, eyeing them for the first time. "We'll be there in two hours." He slid their tickets into the slots above their heads and walked on.

Paul gave a half laugh. He leaned over, his elbows on his knees as he studied the floor. He puffed one cheek out, then the other, tapping his fingertips together. He had a narrow face and deep blue eyes, and Iris had mistaken him for a teenager when he first came into the bookstore where she worked. She liked to look at him when he was most oblivious to her, when he was reading a book, or in the mornings when he was still asleep and there was a sweetness in the warm spaces of his skin. They had been together for five months now.

She took his present out of her bag and quickly placed it on his lap. "Happy birthday!" she exclaimed.

Paul reached over and put his arm around her neck. Iris had to bend forward out of her seat for a kiss. She smiled, though she felt a little awkward with Jeremy watching.

"I was born two hours before midnight," Paul explained to

Jeremy. He stuck a thumb into a crevice of the paper, and the wrapping split open easily. "My doctor was at a party when he got the call and arrived at the hospital in a tuxedo. He wasn't very pleased to see me."

"Do you like it?" Iris asked.

It was an oval black lacquer box that she had found at an antique store on Pine Street. "It's hand-painted from Russia," she told him. On the lid was a night scene of three horses, all different colors—red, white, and brown—gaily pulling a sled. There was a driver holding a gold whip in the air, and two lovers seated in the back of the troika. They were passing through the snow, but the way the ground was painted with its swirls of blue, it seemed to Iris that they were racing magically across the sea. Tiny gold stars shone in the blue-black sky.

"It's very nice," Paul said, lifting the lid to look at the bright red interior. He then picked up the book that she had added at the very last minute.

"Herbert Marcuse," Paul said.

"I'm afraid that was my idea," Jeremy said.

"It's about Freud," Iris said hopefully. She didn't mention that it was a critique of Freud. It had been kind of a joke. She had told Jeremy that Paul was a Freudian, and Jeremy had said, "Maybe we can change that."

"Fantastic," Paul said, but the way he said it slowly, almost ironically, made her feel that she had made a mistake. He turned to Jeremy. "You're going to graduate school for sociology, right?"

"I am," Jeremy replied.

"Where?"

"In California."

"Like it there?"

Jeremy paused. "I do."

"You sound surprised."

"I didn't expect to ever live in California."

"I thought you wanted to study philosophy," Iris said.

"Too impractical," Jeremy said. "It doesn't have any real-world applications. You end up feeling isolated."

"You want to be connected to the world," Iris said, smiling at him. She had not seen Jeremy in two years. He had arrived at her doorstep in Philadelphia the previous night, flushed from the cold. Maybe it was the color in his cheeks, the fact that he had come from outside yet looked so warm in his thick wool sweater, but she thought there was a glow about him that she hadn't seen before. He was different from the way he'd been in high school, when he wore braces and talked slowly, sometimes with a mild stutter. In college, he grew out his hair, wore flannel shirts, and strode around in combat boots with slightly hunched shoulders. He had short hair now, a finely clipped beard, and there was something in the way that he held himself that made him seem more at ease with his own body.

"Has Laura told you?" she said. "She's absolutely in love."

"I've heard," Jeremy replied.

"They met in Chicago." She didn't say anything more, and Paul began to prod Jeremy about Marcuse. Iris thought about Laura as she watched the landscape stream past her window. If she narrowed her eyes, it almost seemed to turn to water. The trees and bracken were the color of dead, wet leaves. They passed the backyards of people's homes, and Iris glimpsed a line of crows sitting on an electric wire, a rusted car without its tires, an orange bicycle left in the snow. She thought about Laura and Erik waiting for them at the station and wondered what kind of man Laura would have fallen in love with, if he would be anything like Paul. Iris had always liked the idea of her and Laura being similar, secretly pleased whenever anyone remarked on their resemblance. Strangers sometimes came up to them, asking if they were sisters. But Laura didn't think they looked at all alike. "People are always confusing one Asian for another," she said.

Over the phone, Laura had told Iris that ever since meeting Erik and moving to New York City she no longer felt as if she were in a state of limbo. Iris wondered about that. The last time she saw Laura was April. They had walked around Laura's neighborhood in Chicago, they had eaten German pancakes sprinkled with lemon juice and powdered sugar, they had gone to the Art Institute to look at photographs by Julia Margaret Cameron. Iris had liked the work, and Laura had found it cloying, and this reaction struck Iris as peculiar, as Laura had always been the idealistic, fanciful one. It was surprisingly cold that day, and after the museum, both of them had felt listless. They wandered around the streets in Lincoln Park, looking inside closed antique stores, at chandeliers and striped settees, mannequins in slightly shabby furs or discolored lace dresses. At one point, Iris stopped and pressed her face against a window, fascinated by a still life with exquisite anatomical flowers. The moribund perfection of the painting disturbed her, especially when she realized that the fly sitting on the tablecloth wasn't real. When she looked up, she saw Laura gazing at the empty street, a blankness in her expression which made Iris want to touch her arm, say something to bring her back, yet she felt exactly as if she were watching Laura behind a pane of glass, and she couldn't speak.

By the time they arrived at Penn Station, Iris was trying to picture how Laura would look when she saw her, but the image that kept appearing in her mind was Laura in her college days when she dyed her hair red and wore translucent, flowery skirts.

Then through the rush of the crowd to find Laura waiting for them in a trim blue coat, black boots, and stockings. She wore a sliver of a barrette in her dark bobbed hair, her hands covered with fur-lined mittens. She and Iris smiled at each other tentatively, and Iris reached out to touch the black fur along Laura's wrist. "Fake," Laura pronounced, pulling off the mitten. "I'm married," she said, holding her hand out to Iris. Everyone looked at the plain silver band on her finger.

"You're kidding," Iris said. "You must be insane!" There was a pause during which she felt everyone looking at her, and she became confused, a sharpness in her voice which she hadn't intended. "Oh, but I mean it in a good way," she said quickly, reaching out to hug Laura. "Congratulations!"

Erik stood silently watching. He had the look of an insomniac, with his slack, unshaven face and drooping hazel eyes. The beige coat he wore was both too short and too wide, probably purchased without fuss at a thrift store. Iris thought his smile, when he did smile, seemed more like a smirk. She didn't think they would have much to say to each other.

She wondered if Jeremy suffered any pang of heart at the news. He had never said anything to Iris, but she knew he was secretly in love with Laura. She watched him now as he pressed Laura's hand, his eyes a deep liquid brown. "I'm happy for you," he said, such kindness in his voice that Iris had to believe it was true.

They spent the afternoon walking around Chinatown and Greenwich Village, going in and out of cafés to keep warm. They ate sushi in a darkly lit restaurant composed of slippery black surfaces where Japanese anime was projected on the wall. It was hallucinatory, Iris thought, watching the radioactive glare of characters as they jumped twenty feet into the air, their mouths opening in perfect circles, though no sound came out. She felt the incongruity of two worlds—the lurid, colorful vision flashing on the walls, and the dark, shining surface of the present moment, of reality, as she watched Laura's nimble fingers fold and refold a napkin until it was the shape of a crane perched along the glossy table.

Iris was struck by Laura's calm. She seemed to take things in moderation, her face open yet peaceful, her entire being as still and clear as a drop of glass. Is that what love did? Iris wondered. Laura had undergone some kind of transfiguration, and there was nothing Iris could do but pretend to be happy for her.

New York was always slightly unnerving to Iris. People looking at you, and you looking back. There seemed to be no end to dissatisfaction and desire. It was easy to look and to want to be someone else, to look and to feel that there was something you lacked. She had this feeling now as people stared at her, shapeless in her winter coat, making her way through a bar in SoHo after Laura. The bodies she pressed against were encased in black, as sleek and beautiful as cockroaches, with martinis dangling from their fingers. Erik had spotted a low table from which people were getting up to leave. He stood beside the sofa, silent and inscrutable, his coat neatly draped over his arm.

The waitress came by to get their orders. Jeremy asked for a Coke.

"You don't want to drink tonight?" Iris asked him. She noticed a woman with slick, coiled hair at the table next to theirs holding a martini glass filled with black liquid. "I want to try what she's having," she said to the waitress.

"Baha'is don't drink," Jeremy told her.

"Oh, right," she said. "Why is it again they don't drink?"

"It clouds the mind. We think you should always be in control of your actions."

"What do Baha'is think about sex?" Paul asked. He was sitting beside Erik, across from them, leaning over the table to hear.

"They don't believe in premarital sex," Jeremy said.

"So you're celibate?"

"Well, no."

"So you have sex, but you don't drink," Paul said. "How do you decide to do one thing and not the other?"

Iris stared at Paul. "He's an atheist," she said to Jeremy. "He likes to pick apart people's religions." She didn't mention that he liked to pick apart people as well. This pleasure of his could be exhausting to Iris, like finding a loose thread and pulling just to see it unravel.

The waitress came back with their drinks. Iris lifted her conical glass, trying to catch the murky light. The black liquid reminded her of ink, and she wondered if it would stain her lips. She took a tentative sip.

"How is it?" Laura asked her.

"Worse than I expected," she said. They smiled at each other. They weren't used to seeing each other with men around. She wondered what Laura thought about Paul. It made her nervous and also excited whenever she caught Laura or Jeremy staring at him. When they watched him, it was as though they were studying her as well, turning her over in their hands to catch a gleam in a surface they hadn't seen reflected before. She supposed she did the same thing to Laura whenever she studied Erik, but Laura never cared what people thought.

"So tell me more," Iris said. "How did it happen so quickly?"

Laura shrugged. "It just seemed like the right time. We both wanted it, that's all."

"And did you tell anyone?"

"Our parents. Erik's mother drove down from Connecticut to be our witness."

Iris wanted to ask Laura why she hadn't been told as well, but she sensed that she was being conventional, trying to impart significance to an event that had nothing to do with her. She touched Laura's arm. "I want to give you something."

"You don't have to."

"But I want to," she said, feeling more excited by her idea. She slipped one earring off and then the other, amethysts surrounded by tiny silver pearls. "Do you remember? I bought these from that man in New Orleans." She looked at them again before pressing the pair into Laura's hand.

Laura was silent as she studied the small gems in her palm. Her face was impassive, her lips slightly pursed. When she tilted her head to put them on, it seemed as if she were making a concession to Iris, for courtesy's sake. She looked at Paul and gave him a knowing smile. "It's ten-seventeen," she announced.

Iris leaned back on the sofa, taking a sip of her drink. Two more hours until the new year. She watched as Laura's fingers traced the rim of her wineglass, her fingers bare except for the silver band on her left hand. Iris wondered what had become of her other rings—the Irish wedding band with the two hands balancing a crown, the red drop of amber with its gold splinters, the lime green stone flecked with pink which looked like a turtle's carapace. It was strange, but Iris felt Laura receding further away from her the more she concentrated on her bare fingers moving over the glass.

Erik got up to go to the restroom, and Laura asked Iris if she wanted to take his seat.

"All right," she said. She got up and sat down next to Paul.

"How are you doing?" he asked her.

"I'm okay," she said. "And you? Are you enjoying yourself?"

"Sure." Paul lowered his voice. "He doesn't talk much, does he? He just sits there and doesn't say a word. Kind of creepy, if you ask me." He pointed his head in Laura's direction. "She's nice, but she has bad teeth."

"Bad teeth." She gave his arm a little shake. She couldn't help but smile, though.

"What?" he said when she looked at him. "I can't help it. I notice these things."

She looked at her friends across the table. Jeremy was showing Laura the sketches he had done while visiting his mother's family in Peru. She had already seen them and thought they were bad, but she was oddly touched by his enthusiasm. "What do you think of Jeremy?" she asked Paul.

"He's interesting, but he's a hypocrite."

"I appreciate him more now," Iris reflected. "In high school, Laura and I used to call him a monster. He always made us feel bad about ourselves."

"Why? What did he do?"

"He was always thinking about the consequences of things. About the larger issues in the world."

"You mean about things other than himself."

She looked at him. He was always trapping her. "I guess," she said. She took hold of his wrist to look at his watch. It was a little past ten-thirty. "You're twenty-four now," she said. "Happy birthday!"

"Yes, that happened about fifteen minutes ago."

"Oh." She was silent for a moment. "Is that why Laura was talking about the time before?"

"Yes."

"How did she know?"

"I told them at the restaurant, remember? I guess she has a better eye for detail than you do."

"I'm sorry. I don't know why I forgot." She grabbed his hand and held it in her lap. "Happy birthday," she said. She bent over to kiss his hand.

"Well, thank you," he said.

"Do you like being born on New Year's Eve?" she asked.

"No, you always end up feeling ripped off."

Iris caught a glimpse of the damp, craggy walls of the tunnel before the subway plunged again into darkness, rattling away as if a piece of it were missing. She liked how the train was moving even though she was sitting still. She was hurtling toward some kind of void, and there was nothing she could do. She sat back in her chair, blinking, staring at the people around her. Beside themselves, there were only three others on the subway, two older men and a woman about her age, all of them alone, spaced out among the empty seats. This moment, this sliver of time, between one year and the next, was so palpable. You were forced to reflect on all you had and hadn't done, and there was always a hope that things would change—or more important, that you would change. What did it all mean? She looked at the strangers' faces, wondering what each of them was thinking, sitting here on a train on New Year's Eve.

"Five more minutes," Paul said, glancing down at his watch.

"Isn't it funny that we're on a train?" she said.

"At least it's heated."

"A train?" Jeremy said. "What's wrong with a train?"

"It's just not the most exciting place to be."

"You want something more exciting than this?" Paul said.

"She gets bored easily," Laura said. "She always likes to be moving about."

Iris laughed. "Am I the only person who thinks we should be somewhere else?" She looked at Erik, but he only looked back at her without saying anything.

"Tell us more about your cousin," Laura said to Jeremy.

"He's an artist. I don't know him that well, actually. And I haven't seen him in two years."

"What kind of pictures does he paint?"

"Abstract things," Jeremy said. "Lots of blues and yellows."

So they were going to a party hosted by a person none of them really knew. At the last minute, they had decided to go to this party, and now they were stuck on a train as it was approaching midnight. She thought about all the people crammed into Times Square who were about to watch the ball drop. She herself had never been to Times Square on New Year's Eve, though she had seen the countdown numerous times on television. It was funny how people never failed to turn on the television at parties she went to. It stemmed from the same desire she had now. People wanted validation of what they were feeling, or needed to absorb some kind of momentum from the crowd, to become part of a current of emotion larger than themselves. It was a way of marking the moment, of trying to sustain a certain level of euphoria. Iris wondered if she would ever become like her parents, who were asleep in their beds by ten p.m. She didn't know which was worse. To be like her parents or the people watching their television sets as the ball dropped.

She looked up and noticed Erik watching her. They regarded each other for a moment, and then he looked away, clearing his throat, his hands folded quietly in his lap. Iris couldn't tell whether his silence was a result of shyness or a feeling of superiority. He had probably murmured no more than twenty words that night to her. She didn't understand how Laura could have fallen in love with him.

"Thirty seconds," Paul said.

She squeezed his hand. "I won't forget this," she told him.

A cigar was perched between their host's fat fingers, and he held a glass of Scotch in the same hand. "Jeremy," he said. "The light of my life. Why are you always materializing out of nowhere? Who are your friends here?" He stared at each of them, sizing up their proportions. He was not a bit like Jeremy, Iris thought. He was large and ponderous, and he had his own atmosphere. Everyone's eyes were on him.

Victor turned to Erik, who was standing next to him. "So what do you do?"

"I kill a lot of rats," Erik said.

"Magnificent," Victor said, nodding his head. "This is a nice group of friends you have, Jeremy. Please enter." He gave a little bow and flourish of his hand.

They dumped their coats and bags in a corner, leaving Jeremy behind as he talked to his cousin. A woman dressed in a Barbarella outfit was swirling ribbons in the air. The ribbons undulated like serpents as the woman rippled them about her body, moving them in circles above her head. In Victor's studio, people had formed small clusters, dotting the room like constellations that grew and then disbanded. As they didn't know anyone, they headed for the food, but they had arrived too late. The table was littered with olive pits and torn husks of bread, soiled napkins and stray plastic cups holding dregs of wine. A yellow formless cheese hardened under the glare of the light, coated with a plastic sheen. Paul poked at the remains of a ham bone, and Erik lifted up empty wine bottles. Iris and Laura abandoned the table, wandering around the studio to look at the people and the paintings. Haphazard streaks of blue and red paint marred the wood floors. They stopped in front of two huge canvases, both of them unfinished, leaning against the wall.

"What do you think?" Laura said.

Iris shrugged. "I don't know. I've never understood modern art." She looked around the room at Victor's paintings, all of them abstract, driven by geometric forms. "I guess they don't do much for me," she finally said.

"I like that one the best." Laura pointed across the room to a layered patchwork of blue and green prisms. "It makes me think of the glass that you pick up on the beach."

Iris tilted her head. "I like your image better than the painting." She turned around to examine the unfinished paintings leaning against the wall. She could see pencil lines on the sections of blank canvas, and it seemed a miracle the way the empty spaces metamorphosed into color. "I like these," she said to Laura. "It makes me see the effort behind it."

Laura smiled. "I thought the point was not to see the effort."

Paul and Erik came up to them, handing them plastic cups filled with red wine. Laura turned toward Erik with a smile.

Her fingers grazed the back of his neck and rested against his collar. Paul was looking at Laura, and Iris wondered if he thought her attractive. She peered over her cup, taking another sip of wine as she studied them. She heard a whir and then a click and turned to see a white-haired woman lowering her camera. "For Victor," the woman said with a smile, moving away to take snapshots of other guests. Iris touched her face, already flushed from the martini. She wondered what Victor would see when he was given the photograph. The four of them standing there as if for an eternity, when already the scene was dissolving, about to disappear. Maybe there would be a time when she would remember this moment, and no one in the photograph would be in her life anymore. It was a possibility.

A young woman with red hair slinked by in a dress that was cut low and plastered to her body. She was thin like Laura, with delicate bones, one of those waifs who could be glimpsed in advertisements, peering at you with hunger.

"Why don't you ever wear things like that?" Paul whispered in her ear.

Iris jabbed his elbow, making him spill a little of his wine.

"Hey," he said, looking down at the floor and then examining his shirt. "You can't take a joke."

She didn't say anything.

"What's wrong with wearing something like that?"

"You're annoying me," she said. She glanced at Laura and Erik, wondering if they could hear, and then she moved away, walking along the table as if looking for something to eat. Paul followed and cut himself a wedge of melted Brie. He offered it to her, and she shook her head.

"So why are you afraid to wear something like that?" he asked.

"You never give up, do you?"

"Are you afraid it would be too 'demeaning'?"

"I wouldn't feel right."

"You don't want people to look at you."

"No, not like that," she said. "What if I told you to begin showing some chest hair?"

"I would if you wanted me to."

"Thanks but no thanks."

"You see?" he said.

She felt a surge of despair rising in her. "I don't see why you're always trying to change me."

"I just think you're afraid of certain things."

"You don't like who I am," she said bitterly.

"You said it, not me," he replied.

She felt her eyes clouding over and blinked as she looked at the woman with red hair laughing across the room. She didn't understand why he enjoyed making her doubt herself. It was hopeless. They always ended up arguing about trivial things. "I don't know why we're together," she said. She felt dizzy moving away from him. A piece of hair hung in her face, and she pulled it behind her ear. Laura and Erik were talking in the corner, their heads bowed close together. Iris didn't feel like joining them and stumbled out of the room. Blood was rushing to her head, and she felt things slowing down, as if her ears were plugged with cotton and the world was far away.

Someone grabbed her wrist, and she looked up. "Want to dance, Iris?" Jeremy said.

She looked at him dimly. "I can't dance."

"No matter," Jeremy said, and he pulled her to the dance floor.

They were playing rumba music. Jeremy knew the dance, and she tried to follow his steps. He spun her around, and she laughed. Her arms and legs were loose and formless, as if made of Jell-O. "You're good at this!" she shouted over the music.

"I love to dance," he said, smiling. He moved his hips suggestively, and she laughed again.

"You've really blossomed," she told him. Once the words were out of her mouth, she realized she was drunk.

"Blossomed?" he said to her.

"I mean you've changed, you've found yourself." She knew she sounded like an idiot. "You know what I mean. It's a compliment."

He only smiled at her. The dance was over, and they walked back to Laura and Erik. Paul was there too, but she didn't look at him.

"You two looked good up there," Paul said, taking a sip of his wine.

She stared down at her feet. "I think I need to use the restroom."

"I'll go with you," Laura said.

They found the bathroom at the end of the hallway, but someone was already waiting by the door. Iris leaned against the wall, closing her eyes for a second only. When she opened them, she asked Laura what married life was like.

"What do you mean?" Laura said.

"I mean, do you feel like you've been transformed? That life is suddenly pulsing with meaning?"

"It's not that dramatic," Laura said.

Then what is it? she wanted to say. But she was silent. She hated how Laura didn't tell her things anymore. Laura's face had the bland smoothness of eggshells, perfectly sealed off. She had retreated behind a calmness that spoke of the great change in her life, a change that did not include Iris.

"I can't explain it," Laura said, slowly turning the ring around her finger. "Things are more simple now."

"How so?"

"It's just a feeling I have." Laura looked up, and Iris was struck by the plain color of her eyes. She no longer wore colored contacts, the ones that gave her eyes a gray-green translucence. It was an otherworldly hue, which Iris once resented and now oddly missed. "I used to feel outside of things," Laura said. "As if I were waiting for something. But now I wake up in the mornings, and I'm just there, I'm happy. I don't want to be anywhere else. I've never felt like that before."

Iris didn't know what to say. She imagined Laura and Erik shut up together in a little room, not wanting anyone else but each other, and the thought depressed her. In high school, she and Laura had retreated to each other's bedrooms, locking the door against the mundane world of school and parents. Laura would light a few candles on her night table and dresser, and immediately it felt as if they had entered their own realm. They sat on her bed or sprawled along the floor, and they talked until morning. What did they talk about? Iris couldn't remember exactly, but the room would be alive and glowing. There were the seashells that Laura had lined against the windowsill and the enameled teacups from which they drank. Laura's bead necklaces coiled together in a shallow dish by her cloisonné turtles and tiny glass figurines. They stayed awake until dawn, waiting for the moment when the sky turns dark blue, as if lit from within, like stained glass. "The blue hour," Laura said, looking outside the window. The sky whitened, the room laid bare by colorless light. Out of the silence, the hysterical twittering of birds. The room always seemed colder, emptier, when she blew out the candles.

"It's funny, isn't it?" Laura said.

"What is?" she asked.

"You and me. That we should be happier now. You have Paul, and I have Erik."

"I guess," she said. She didn't tell Laura that she didn't feel she had anyone. They were silent for a while. There was a sound of flushing, and the door opened. A short man came out of the bathroom, and the woman in front of them went in.

"But what will you do when he's no longer there?" Iris said. Laura gazed at her, not understanding. "I mean, don't you ever think about what will happen if he's not there?"

"Why should I think that?"

"Isn't it scary to depend entirely upon another person for your happiness?" Iris said. "What if he goes away?"

"That won't happen," Laura said.

"Well, what if something happens to him?"

"What do you mean? Do you mean if he dies or something?"

"Yeah," she said. "I don't mean to be morbid, but a person dies sometime or another."

Laura looked at her. "I don't think about that."

Iris's cheeks were flaming now. When she went into the bathroom, she saw that her face was red all over, as if she had a sunburn. It was worse on her body, splotches all over her arms and stomach, as if the ugliness inside of her had erupted onto her skin.

Laura was waiting for her outside. They walked through the apartment until they found the men hanging out in the kitchen. The room was lit with candles, creating shadows as they poured themselves more wine from the bottles scattered over the table. There were a few other people sitting around, a couple nestled in the back and three women chatting on the stairs. Paul pulled a wooden chair out next to him. He patted the seat, telling her to sit down. She did, feeling very limp and tired. He smoothed her hair gently with his fingers, circling his hand around the back of her neck.

"Do you want to try a pot brownie?" Paul asked her.

"Sure," she said numbly. "Where did you get them?"

"Victor's wife was going around with a plate full of them while you were in the bathroom."

He handed her a brownie, and she took a large bite.

"This is my third one," he said.

"They taste awful."

"They're not that bad."

"They're bitter," she said. "They taste just like grass."

"Just eat, and don't complain," Paul said.

She took a few more bites. "I want to gag."

"You're such a brat," he said.

She finished the brownie, and she moved closer to him, laying her head upon his shoulder. He put his arm around her, and she closed her eyes.

It was after four in the morning. She wanted nothing more than to be asleep in a warm bed. Yet they were outside, bracing themselves against the icy air, walking—endlessly walking—as coffee-colored houses rose into view, shaping themselves against the edges of her face. She felt like a mummy with her scarf wrapped up over her nose, her eyes tearing from the wind.

She followed the others mindlessly, walking down the stairs to the subway station. Outside, there was inhuman cold that gleamed from the sky. Yet as soon as she descended, she was in an underworld of bodily odors, stinking breath and piss, the floor sticky under her feet.

They waited on the platform under an electric glare, with no wind, though her breath came out like a plume of smoke that faded into the air. Paul was leaning against her, both hands in his pockets, staring at the tracks. He kept tightening and then relaxing his jaw, as if he were concentrating on something hard. She snapped her fingers once in front of his face. He blinked, shaking his head. "Sorry," he muttered. His eyes were glazed.

"How are you feeling?" she asked.

"Mmmmhhh," he said, nodding.

"What time is it?" she asked Laura.

Laura looked at Erik. "A quarter to five," he said. He stared straight ahead without consulting a watch.

"How do you know?" Iris asked.

"He can always tell what time it is," Laura said. "Give or take fifteen minutes," she added.

"Really?"

"He has an innate sense of time."

She wondered if Laura was pulling her leg. Everyone except her and Paul seemed remarkably sober and awake. "I don't believe you," Iris said. She thought she saw a flicker of a smile pass over Erik's face.

"You're very ironic," she said to Erik. This seemed to startle him, and he gazed back at her. "You always seem to be laughing at other people."

"I don't mean to be," Erik answered.

The train arrived, screeching by. It was half-full, and she and Paul sat down in the first seats they saw, though the others made their way to the back of the car. She felt instinctively that the others avoided them, though it was true there weren't any empty seats close by. She didn't care. She was receding further into a haze. She pressed her head against Paul's shoulder.

"This is the last time I'm doing this," he muttered.

She closed her eyes. Her mind floated in a sea of jelly. Words slipped away and were lost forever. "Why is that?" she heard herself say.

"I don't like how I feel," he said.

"But it's good to feel something different."

"Not like this."

The train rattled underneath her. For a moment, she felt herself falling into empty space. She started, opening her eyes. Paul's jacket was wet where her mouth had been. She was not sure how long she had been sleeping. "Did you say something?" she asked him.

She looked up and saw that his eyes were closed. He looked like a child with his mouth hanging open. She put his hand in her lap, stroking his fingers. She smoothed out his palm and gazed at the surface of his skin. She followed a line, and it would split into other lines, his palm etched with infinite needles. Beneath the lines that crossed and curved along his skin was a fainter network that you could see only in the light, where it dissolved into a translucent terrain. His fingers caught her own, closing with silent life. When she looked at him again, his eyes were half open as though he were watching her. But she realized with shock that he was asleep. His eyes were glassy blue and strange. She had never seen him like this, staring at her from unconscious depths. She felt as if she were peering into something he wouldn't want her to see. He will look like this when he is dead, she thought. Someone tapped her on the shoulder.

"We're getting off here," Laura said.

Iris shook his shoulder. "Paul," she whispered. He jerked his head, blinking. Then he followed her off the train.

Outside, her head seemed to clear a bit. Yet she realized her thoughts were constantly slipping out from under her before she could fix them in place. The streets were empty, and the wind swept through them as if touching nothing. The houses stood frozen and distilled of color, cardboard shadows settling into the ground.

He leaned against her, limping slightly. The others walked on ahead of them.

"Goddamn these shoes," he muttered.

"Do they hurt?" she said.

"I guess they're not broken in. We walked so much today."

Iris felt slightly guilty. He had worn the shoes to please her. She had told him he looked like a teenager when he wore sneakers. "How much farther?" she yelled to Laura. The three of them were at least a block ahead.

"Not too far," Laura called back, her voice ringing clear. "About seven more blocks."

"Only seven," Paul said, grimacing.

"Your poor feet," she said. "I'm sorry."

He grabbed her by the waist, though both of them were puffed out and shapeless in their winter coats. They staggered down the sidewalk together.

"Did you have a nice birthday?" she asked. "Are you glad you came up here?"

"Yes, I liked your friends."

"Did you?" She didn't tell him that she was feeling left out of her own circle. She wondered why Jeremy chose to stick around Laura and Erik. The two of them had been drinking, yet they managed to stay clearheaded, while she and Paul hung over each other's shoulders, tottering around like adolescents.

"I don't know if they liked me," Paul said.

She didn't say anything, and they walked for another block without speaking.

"I'm guessing by your silence that they didn't." There was a plaintive note in his voice which startled Iris, and she was at a loss as to what to say. There was such a distance between them. Neither of them seemed to understand the same things.

"I don't know," she said slowly. "I can't really tell what they think."

"You know," he said. "You just don't want to tell me."

They walked on. She bit her lip, staring at the ground rising in waves beneath her feet.

"So you're just going to continue being silent?" he burst out.

She looked at him helplessly. "What can I say?" She didn't want to admit it, but she was vaguely ashamed of him. She felt sorry for him in the same way that she felt sorry for herself.

The others stood in front of the apartment building, waiting for them to catch up. Laura let them inside, and Iris followed her up three flights of stairs and down a narrow corridor with uneven brown tiles. All the while, she could hear Paul talking to Jeremy. "I don't understand her," he was saying. "Do you understand her?" Iris flushed, moving more quickly ahead.

The place was unbelievably ugly to her, senseless in its design. The walls were made of dreary cinder blocks and petrified layers of paint. At what seemed to be a dead end, they found a door and climbed another flight of stairs. A couple of trash bags were wilting in the hallway. "The neighbors always do that," Laura said as she got out her key.

Inside the apartment, several blankets were spread out on the floor. "You and Paul can sleep there," Laura said. The foam mattress in the corner, which she told them she and Erik had purchased that same morning, was for Jeremy. Iris looked around the empty room. There was a brand-new map of the world taped to the wall above a desk and a chair. Beside the desk, a small bookcase. That was all.

"What happened to all your things?" Iris asked.

"They're at my parents' house," Laura said.

"Why didn't you bring them up here?"

Laura shrugged. "It didn't seem necessary."

"Can I see your bedroom?"

"Sure, but there's not much to see."

Iris peeked in and saw a mattress on the floor and a television propped on a crate. There were some clothes scattered on the bed and carpet. It was odd that Laura had gotten rid of most of her stuff. She had always been an aesthete, arranging her objects with care, each element positioned perfectly as in a still life. But it didn't seem to matter to her any longer. The room was anonymous and could have belonged to anyone.

Laura handed them towels, pointing to the bathroom. "Good night," she said, giving Iris a little wave as she shut the bedroom door.

In the bathroom, Iris flicked on the light, and it hummed as she stared at herself in the mirror. Her eyes were bloodshot, her skin dull and blotchy with violet shadows. She washed her face in warm water, ran the toothbrush against her teeth in a perfunctory way. The toilet was an institutional kind with a metal lever. She stepped on it with her shoe, and the toilet flushed violently, shreds of paper spewing back to the surface.

When she came out, she saw Paul lying on top of the blankets. He gazed at her, looking disoriented, but he slowly got to his feet and stumbled to the bathroom. She slipped in under two of the blankets, leaving one comforter to lie on top of. The floor was hard under her back, but she felt blissfully warm as she stretched out her legs.

"Jeremy," she said.

"Uh-huh?" he said.

"Are you going to brush your teeth?"

"I should."

"Why don't you get it over with?"

"Paul's in the bathroom, isn't he?"

"Use the kitchen sink."

"That would be rude."

"Really?"

"Yes, Iris."

"What do you think of Laura's apartment?"

He was silent for a moment. "It's bare and functional."

"Don't you think it's strange?"

"It's very empty," he said.

"It makes you wonder how much she's changed," Iris said.

"She no longer needs the same things."

"I miss her candles and books," she sighed. "The poems that she hung along the wall."

"Yes," he said. He didn't say anything more, and she let him drift off to sleep. She lay quietly on the floor, looking at the darkened window. In another hour, the sky would lighten, turn incandescent blue, but she did not have the heart to wait for it.

She heard Paul open the bathroom door, flick off the light. He got underneath the blankets and sighed, murmuring her name. He reached out for her in the dark. His breath was in her neck and in her hair, and her hips cracked when he lay on top of her. He kissed her gently on the tip of her nose three times. She smiled. It was sweet. His desire moved her in ways she couldn't understand. She felt it there, below her stomach. But when he pressed against her, his hands beneath her shirt, she didn't move. She wanted to, but she was afraid Jeremy was awake, listening. Paul's lips were against her own, and she felt as if they were floating, their mouths touching like fishes' mouths, cold and wet, as they breathed into each other. But she lay very still, pretending to be asleep. He stopped, touching her face once with the tips of his fingers before moving away to the other side. In silence, she waited until she could hear the sound of his breathing, low and steady in the darkness.

TRANSPARENCY

Henry Liu lost his voice halfway through the trip, coughing so violently that he thought he pulled a muscle on his left side. Whenever he felt pain, he put his hand across his chest to reassure himself that his heart was still beating. He looked at the view as his wife drove, at the broken edges of mountains covered in snow and the turquoise lake where not a single fish lived because of its cold waters. The mountains held a stillness that silenced him. It moved him to think how many thousands of years they had stood, worn silently away by wind and ice, and he felt regret as the lake slipped past his window. When it disappeared from view, Henry felt as if he had been given a last glimpse of the world. He knew that he would be dead before the trip was over.

His sixteen-year-old son, James, slouched in his seat, playing his Game Boy. Alice leaned her head against the window, reading a Russian novel for college — it was a thousand pages at the very least — by an author whose name Henry couldn't pronounce. His wife kept exclaiming at the scenery — *look out-*

side, isn't it beautiful?—and when neither of their children looked, she became angry, saying what a waste it had been to bring them, until their daughter put the novel down on her knee and gazed through the window. His wife drove the car in fits and starts, pressing down hard on the accelerator and just as suddenly releasing it so that the car kept lurching forward and then slowing down. "Mom," James yelled, "you're making me sick! Stop it!"

"What?" she said.

"Your driving! It sucks! I'm a better driver, right, Alice?"

Alice picked up her novel and flipped a page.

"Mom, stop the car and let me drive!"

"You shut up," Henry's wife said. "I don't want all of us to end up dead at the bottom of the cliff."

James gave a heavy sigh as he collapsed back into his seat. He glanced out the window. "Everything looks the same," he complained. He picked up his Game Boy and pushed his glasses back with the edge of a finger.

Henry rolled down his window, but his wife turned to look at him. She didn't like the wind hitting her face because the lady who sold her makeup said that moving air wasn't good for her complexion. So he closed the window, and they drove like that for another hour or so, the rented car smelling of vinyl, the way new cars smell, and lukewarm air blowing in softly through the vents. Through the glass, Henry stared at the mountains taking up the sky, massive fissured surfaces that from a distance became faint blue outlines. He wanted to remember them, but it seemed impossible for his mind to remember anything so beautiful and vast. On previous vacations, he had bought a postcard or two to remind him of the places they had seen, but this attempt at memory now seemed like wasted effort.

A tickle crept into his throat, and Henry held his breath. He didn't want to begin coughing, but the itch blossomed until he felt he was suffocating. His eyes watered as he hunched over in his seat, coughing. His family watched him in silence. "How are you?" his wife finally asked.

Henry nodded, swallowing, his fingers touching his throat.

"Your father is sick." His wife sounded surprised, as though she hardly believed it. Ever since Henry had lost his voice, his family talked about him as if he weren't there. What about Dad? his children would say. Poor Dad! Their regard made Henry feel his sickness even more. He would look at the lines of his skin, its cracked translucence, and wonder if he were becoming invisible.

His children liked to hear him croak. "He sounds like the Godfather," James said. "Hey, Dad! Can you say 'He sleeps with the fishes.' Say it, Dad." Henry just smiled. When he wore his gray jacket and pants, James and Alice addressed him as Don. "How's it going, Don?" they said, and laughed together in the backseat of the car. They made their voices deep and scratchy. "You do a favor for me, I'll do a favor for you."

It was odd, but when he did speak, his family stopped their chatter and listened to his every syllable. He spoke so rarely that his words seemed to hold unusual power. Now, as they followed a winding road through the mountains, Henry lifted his hand up. His wife glanced at him. "Stop," he said. His voice was like dry wind, he felt his insides shaking. His wife pulled over to the side.

"Are you okay, Dad?" Alice asked.

"Okay," he whispered. "Water."

Alice found a bottle underneath a jacket on the floor and poured him a cup. Henry drank quickly with everyone watching. When he was done, he pointed to the mountains outside the window and then opened the car door to get out.

"What's he doing?" Alice asked.

"Dad's going crazy!" James said.

"He wants to see the view," his wife told them.

His wife and Alice got out and followed him to the overlook while James stayed inside the car. Henry stepped onto a large red rock to see the view. "Let me get a picture," Alice said to her mother. "Smile!" Her voice was buoyant in the singsong way of people who are taking photographs. Henry noticed that his wife was smiling without really smiling. Her face seemed to be resisting the wind. She kept blinking as she held her lips together, a colorful silk scarf surrounding her throat. Henry was struck by how old she looked as she waited for Alice to take the photograph. "Dad, turn around," Alice said. Henry shook his head without looking at her, waving his hand as if brushing away a fly. His daughter took his picture anyway, a side profile of him gesticulating on top of the rock.

"Why doesn't he want his picture taken?" Alice asked her mother.

"Don't worry about him," his wife said. She and Alice paused for a moment, breathing in the view. "So beautiful!" his wife sighed. Then they turned and headed back to the car.

Henry set one foot on top of another rock. A burned oak tree rose from the craggy earth, its limbs twisted in the air. Acorns hung from the dried-up branches, as colorless as silver. They looked petrified, and Henry thought it remarkable that they had not already fallen. He picked up a small piece of rock, brick red, like a misshapen diamond, and pressed it into his palm. One side was crusted with dirt, leaving his fingers dusty and dry. It smelled like stale smoke, like ash, when he sniffed at it.

When he looked back to where the car was parked, he noticed that his family was staring at him. He tossed the rock to the ground and then spat along the side of the road, trying to clean his tongue of its acrid taste. When he was inside the car again, before they had driven even a mile, he turned to his wife, speaking to her in Chinese. "Please take me to the hospital," he said.

Three hours passed by as they waited in the emergency room for a doctor. Henry had complained of chest pain, so the nurse had taken his blood pressure and pulse to make sure he wasn't having a heart attack. She also drew a sample of his blood and sent it to the laboratory. His wife had dropped their children off at a tour company after giving them permission to sign up for an ATV ride. Henry didn't like the idea at all, but his wife relented after James promised he wouldn't drive but would share a vehicle with his sister. Henry knew, of course, that Alice would let her brother drive, but he didn't say anything to stop them.

There was a television in the waiting room, and he and his wife were watching the men's finals at Wimbledon. The screen was mounted so high, however, that it was impossible to follow the ball as it flew across the net. After squinting for an hour, Henry finally gave up and closed his eyes, while his wife continued to watch. He was tired of the heartless drama and the crowd, which demanded nothing less than perfection from the players.

With his eyes closed, Henry concentrated on the pain inside his throat. He wanted to drink something—hot tea with a couple of cough drops thrown in, a few tablespoons of whiskey mixed with honey and lemon—anything to relieve the soreness. The air had turned raw in his throat, as if he were breathing particles of dust. He had heard of people struggling with asthma being able to breathe again after being submerged in water, and he thought once more about the lake he had seen that afternoon, its glacial stillness with not a single thing stirring below. He imagined lying on the silt floor, his nameless body edged in blue, drifting without words or sound along the empty bottom.

His wife shook his arm, and Henry woke. He cleared his throat and sat up straight in his chair. Several people were looking at him. "You were snoring," his wife told him. His body felt cold and damp, and he rose shakily to his feet. "Where are you going?" his wife asked.

He pointed his thumb toward the window.

"Huh?"

"Outside," he muttered.

In front of the hospital, there were a few empty benches. Henry chose the one facing the most sunlight and blinked as he sat down. The sun felt weak against his skin, as though the light were passing through him.

"You have a smoke?"

Henry looked up at a woman standing beside him. She was in her early thirties with frizzy brown hair, and she wore the flimsy gown issued to patients. When she stepped in front of him, Henry could see that she wore another gown underneath, reversed to cover her back. Her right arm was attached to an IV drip, and she had dragged the metal stand along the cement walkway with her.

"What?" Henry asked.

"Do you have a smoke?" she repeated. She made the motions of taking a cigarette in and out of her mouth.

Henry shook his head, waving his hand.

A nurse wearing blue scrubs walked through the sliding doors and approached him. "Henry Liu?" she asked.

Henry nodded, getting up out of his seat.

"Actually, Mr. Liu, you can stay where you are. I just wanted to check on how you're doing."

"Okay."

"We're almost ready to see you. We're still waiting for the results from the lab. It won't be more than an hour or so."

"Nurse," the woman said, "got a smoke?"

"I'm afraid not," the nurse said, turning away.

"God, what does it take to get a cigarette around here?" the woman demanded. She paced up and down the walkway with the IV stand. She stopped by his bench and rubbed her shoe along the cement curb. "This feels nice. Henry, right?"

Henry looked over at her in surprise.

"Henry," the woman said again, "won't you talk to me?"

Henry tapped the base of his throat and shook his head.

"I know my body better than any doctor," the woman said, "but they won't let me smoke. I can't even drink my glasses of water. You know what they call my condition? Psychogenic polydipsia. 'Psycho-fucking-what?' I said. Who would think water could be bad for you?"

Henry raised his eyebrows and looked at her.

"My ions are off," she said. "Missing electrolytes. The doctor said I was drowning."

The woman's eyes had a green fluorescence. When she spoke, the skin around her mouth moved tightly, as if she'd received a face-lift. Yet she couldn't have been older than thirty-five or so.

"You don't believe me, do you?" the woman said. "You probably think I need a new liver or something."

Henry cleared his throat. "How much water . . . ?" He curled his fingers and made the gesture of drinking from an imaginary cup.

"A lot, Henry. I am addicted to water. The pills I take make my mouth so dry." A couple walked toward them from the parking lot. "Hey, excuse me, got a smoke?" the woman yelled.

"Sorry," the man said, and the couple passed by.

The woman pulled her IV stand closer to the bench and sat down beside Henry. "Guess how much water I drink."

Henry shrugged.

"Come on, guess."

In his lap, Henry stuck out his thumb and forefinger. "Two gallons," he whispered.

"No," the woman said. "I drink four hundred and forty-eight fluid ounces each day. Three and a half gallons of water." The woman leaned her head back, tapping her fingers along the bench, paying no mind to the tube that came out of her hand. She crossed her legs, bobbing one foot up and down, the laces of her tennis shoe dangling. Henry could see short brown hairs sprouting from her legs. His wife didn't ever need to shave; her legs were so dry that they had a sheen to them, like cracked porcelain.

"Nothing more delicious," the woman said. "Everything has a taste except water. You know how hard it is to find something without a taste, Henry?" She began fiddling with the intravenous tube on the back of her hand. "The other night I dreamed I was sitting in a restaurant with my ex-husband, Ronny, and it was like we were married all over again. The only thing he said to me was 'I've flushed out my ears.' Then he proceeded to cut his bread into small pieces. To be honest, I was more interested in looking at the menu. There were fancy things, a lot of French words I didn't know. But I remember one dish in particular. Encrusted Squab Stuffed with Goat

Cheese. Can you imagine? All I wanted was meat loaf, but I couldn't find it on the menu. The more I looked, the more convinced I was it was my last meal." The woman caressed her IV with the tips of her fingers. It made Henry nervous, worried that she might yank the tube out at any moment. "I never wanted to have a taste for things."

"*Lou* Liu," a voice said from behind. Henry jerked his head up, saw that his wife was standing behind the bench. Old man, she had called him. Old Liu. His wife stared at the woman sitting beside him.

"Your wife, Henry?" the woman said.

Henry got up awkwardly out of his seat. He would have introduced them, but he didn't know the woman's name.

"It's time for me to pick up the kids," his wife said to him in Chinese.

"Oh, I know," the woman said. "That's Japanese, isn't it?"

"Okay," he said. "I'll be here waiting."

"What are you talking about, Henry?" the woman asked.

"Who is that?" his wife said, digging through her purse. Henry shrugged. His wife put on her sunglasses. "Don't forget about insurance," she said as she turned away. She walked to the parking lot, clutching her purse. Henry watched her recede into a horizon of glinting cars.

"Well, I have a better chance of understanding you when you don't say anything at all," the woman said when Henry sat down again. "How long have you been married, Henry?"

The question startled him. He stared down at his feet planted on the smooth, newly laid walkway. For his last birthday, his wife had to remind him that he was turning fifty-three, not fifty-two as he had thought. Sometimes he caught himself drifting only to be seized with panic that he no longer knew where he was. The years had passed by as in a dream, and he suddenly found himself sitting on this bench, speaking to a woman he didn't know, as he tried to remember his life.

"Twenty-two," he finally answered.

"Impressive," the woman remarked. "Ronny and I didn't last half that long. Love can turn ugly so fast. The simplest things about him made me go crazy. Like at night, when Ronny brushed his teeth, he used this curved metal thing to scrape his tongue. He liked showing me all the gunk it collected and tried to persuade me to use it. Whenever we went out to eat, he'd inspect his glass. If there was the slightest water spot, he'd wipe it down with a napkin." The woman sighed. "It's the stupid, small things that make you hate someone. We parted ways, and then last summer a neighbor found Ronny. I never thought he would be capable of doing that. He didn't leave a note, just a piece of paper calculating how much he would have to fall. He was a hundred eighty-nine pounds, and he worked it out that he would have to fall eight feet and two inches." The woman scratched her elbow.

"I know what you're thinking," she said, folding her hands over her stomach. "The doctors ask me all the time. Do you know what's going to happen to you if you don't stop? they say. Seizures. Coma. I don't know whether to believe them or not. I have such a terrible thirst." The woman paused to gaze at Henry. "You don't think my body would be steering me wrong, do you?"

The skin along the woman's face sagged once she stopped talking. Henry wondered what it would mean to be like her, smoking her cigarettes, taking her pills, drinking her water. He had never been addicted to anything in his life. He imagined her arranging glasses of water neatly in a row. She would pick up a glass and begin to drink, and when it was empty she would pick up another, letting the liquid pour down her throat, filling the folds of her stomach. She was trying to drown something inside of her, but Henry didn't think it could be done.

"It's the moments of pettiness that you regret," the woman said, "even though they reveal who you really are."

When the nurse came to get him, he rose out of his seat.

"So long, Henry." The woman smiled. She gave him her hand, brown and lithe, the nails bitten down to shapeless stubs. Her skin had a soft dryness, and her fingers clutched his own with nervous energy. He turned and followed the nurse back inside.

After taking his vital signs — measuring his temperature and pulse, his blood pressure, respiratory rate, and oxygen saturation — after taking his blood and submitting it to a laboratory for tests, after giving him a chest X-ray and then a CAT scan, hooking him up to the cardiac monitor to follow the rhythms of his heart, it was determined that Henry had bronchitis. Henry laughed at the news. It wasn't too serious, the doctor said, prescribing for him the usual course of antibiotics as well as a cough syrup with codeine to suppress the fits and relieve the pain. Henry's family was sitting in the waiting room when he came down the hallway. He had a bracelet around his wrist, and he was holding a white paper bag containing his medications.

"What's up, Don?" his son said to him.

"How are you doing, Dad?" Alice asked.

Henry nodded his head and smiled. He'd taken his antibiotics and cough syrup already and felt like he was going to be better. "You drive?" he asked his son.

"Sure," James said.

"We saw a bear from the side of the road," Alice told him.
Henry's eyes widened. "A bear!"

"He had a white patch on his chest," Alice said. "He stood up on his hind legs when he saw us."

"Alice tried to take his picture," James said, "but he ran into the forest when he saw her."

"You kids." He smiled, patting his son on the shoulder.

Outside, the mountains had become a mass of shadows darker than the sky. Henry felt them closing in as their tiny car pressed forward along the highway. They stopped at a seafood restaurant a few miles from their motel. Henry wanted to eat for the first time in several days and ordered two bowls of vegetable soup. Alice had brought her novel into the restaurant— she was at a good part, she explained, and had only a couple of pages left in the chapter. She read diligently until the food came and then placed her book facedown on the tablecloth.

Henry cleared his throat. "What kind of story?" he asked, pointing to the cover of his daughter's book.

"Oh!" Alice exclaimed. "It's hard to say." She bit her lip, revealing her large opalescent teeth. "It's about this young man who's innocent. Almost like a saint," she said, touching the spine of her book thoughtfully. "He's in love with a general's daughter, but there's also this tortured, fallen woman. She's beautiful and mad, all these men are in love with her, but she doesn't like any of them. One of them gives her a hundred thousand rubles, but she throws them into the fire."

"Sounds like a stupid book," James said.

"It's not," Alice said.

His wife cut off a piece of her salmon and put it onto Henry's plate for him to try. Henry couldn't help but notice the gentle slope of her hands, her maternal fingers and clear, rounded nails. They had been at an ice-skating rink, he remembered, when he first touched her hand. She had clung to the wall, wearing a bright yellow dress—a dress, even though they were skating!—but he realized she had worn it for him, and as she tottered on her skates, he had taken her small cold fingers into his own.

His wife's jade bracelet gleamed in the light as she turned her wrist. The waiter came and refilled their glasses of water. Henry touched his glass, felt the beads of condensation along his fingertips. He thought of the woman at the hospital, imagined her lying awake at this hour, trying to forget the dryness in her mouth. Perhaps she swallowed her own saliva for relief, moistening her lips with her tongue. He lifted the glass to his mouth, his lips parted to receive its coolness.

Something clinked against his teeth. A pink mass floated up toward his lips.

"Dad, my water!" James laughed.

Henry saw a pink retainer sitting in the glass he was holding. His family erupted into laughter.

"I put it in there for a rinse," James said.

"You know your father is getting confused," his wife said.

"I didn't see," Alice laughed. "Did he really drink from it?"

People began looking over at their table. Henry flushed, realizing that he was still holding the glass of water in his hand. He felt a painful throb in his chest, as if his heart were swollen, but he knew that it would be years before it finally gave out. He could hear it beating louder and louder now as he set the glass on the table and waited for his family to quiet down.

SONATA FOR
THE LEFT HAND

I. Palm Reading

In July, before the levees broke in New Orleans, my friend Kate and I had our palms read in Jackson Square. We arrived in the city after a tropical storm. Thousands had lost electricity, and beautiful old trees had fallen. We were there to attend our friend Sylvia's wedding, and there was news that a hurricane might hit that weekend. "We never get tropical storms this time of year," Sylvia told us. "So bizarre. I hope Friday stays nice and dry."

On Friday, Kate and I sipped café au lait as the rain poured down in sheets. We were sitting under the huge awning at Café du Monde, and bedraggled pigeons pecked at our feet. The floor was heavily dusted with powdered sugar, and the pigeons looked as unhealthy as could be—what you might expect from a diet consisting of powdered beignets. We were sorry for Sylvia and her spoiled wedding, but in an hour the downpour had stopped and the sun was out again. It was so hot we could see steam rising from the sidewalks.

We walked along Decatur Street past the fortune-teller stands in Jackson Square, and Kate glanced at me with a doubtful smile that was at once ironic and full of longing. The fortune-tellers sensed Kate's need and offered her a reading for ten dollars. "Go ahead," I encouraged her, and she presented her palm with sad, hopeful resignation to a gypsy woman whose sign declared that she had thirty-seven years of palmistry experience.

"My dear," the gypsy woman said immediately, "you are too obsessed with love. Your preoccupation has been with love, my dear, and your mind has been clouded. You need more sense, my dear. Men are a dime a dozen, and you need to hurt them before they hurt you. Forget them, my dear. They aren't worth your love. You need to focus on other things. Have you ever thought about going into the medical profession?" Kate stared at her blankly. "You write perhaps?" Kate nodded. "Keep writing and focus on that. Start finishing things and begin acting with your head, my dear, instead of your heart."

When the gypsy woman had finished, she regarded me with sharp, humorous eyes. "And you, my dear?" Her face, with its thick, glossy skin, was the color of apricots, and her fingernails were painted a muddy orange. I shook my head, reluctant to part with ten dollars, but Kate and I had not walked a block before I regretted it. The gypsy woman didn't seem surprised when we showed up at her stand again, and I smiled and gave her both my hands.

"You have a bright aura," she said, looking at me and smoothing my left palm. "And you are not one to cry over spilled milk, though you have suffered a recent disappointment, I see. He was not the right one for you, my dear. You are going to marry a businessman in two and a half years. He will be rich, my dear, even though you don't care about money. And you will have three children, one quickly after the other. I know, my dear," she said when she saw my face fall, "you are not patient with children. I know this, but you will have three."

Such was the fate the gypsy woman condemned me to. I felt a certain satisfaction that my life would turn out so dull. "A businessman!" I said merrily. "Three children!"

Kate sighed. "Sometimes I think arranged marriages would have suited me just fine. I like the idea of being handed someone and having no other options. It would save me time and a lot of worry. A man gives you a sign, he emits his little light, and you move toward him, but then he just flickers off, and you're left in the dark again. It's like trying to catch a firefly."

"Or a cab on a rainy day," I said.

Kate mused. "Is a man more like a cab or a firefly?"

That evening Sylvia was married in City Park with three red roses in her hair. We felt a drop or two on our arms, and the sun weaved fitfully in and out of the clouds, but a storm did not break over our heads and everyone commented on the luck of the newlyweds. It seemed fitting that Sylvia, a passionate exhibitionist who was born on Valentine's Day, should be married between a tropical storm and a hurricane, possessing such grace as to be touched by neither.

The reception was held at the groom's home, but because there had been no electricity in the neighborhood for four days, the family had been forced to rent generators. Neighbors had come to their aid and donated fans, and these were spread out around the yard and inside the house. Kate and I sat outside at a long table lit with candles, and it was pleasant to eat crawfish gumbo and sip cold champagne, our dresses stirred by the blowing fans. Everyone spoke loudly over the drone of the generators, and now and then I heard the intimate whine of a mosquito and slapped at my bare shoulders.

We gathered inside the house for a slide show. Photographs of Sylvia and her husband from the time they were children were projected one after another onto the wall. A little Sylvia wearing her mother's sunglasses sitting on a beach. A young Dan sticking his hand in the mouth of a plastic shark. Photographs of them in Halloween costumes, smiling with their families, sporting bell-bottoms, new perms, braces. A delightful naïveté shone on their faces, for how were they to know what was coming and who they were going to love? It was a story of two lives coming together, and I thought the slide show made a convincing case for the hand of fate.

I couldn't help but think of Vincent, whose childhood photos I had never seen. A few weeks ago, we had parted ways, and now I felt a bitterness rise up within me at the thought of his family, who would always be dear to him, who would always be in his life, whereas I was shut out of it. The last time I had seen him, we had taken a walk together along the narrow country road that ran in front of my house, and I had explained that I loved him and he said he felt nothing at all. Two large dogs came running out from a neighboring farm, trailing beside us and barking. The dogs began chasing each other, and one of them knocked into Vincent, who stumbled and fell. "Oh, my dear!" I said, reaching my hand toward him, but he moved away and got up off the road by himself. I couldn't understand it. He had loved me once, and now he couldn't even bear to touch my hand.

Toward midnight, Sylvia rushed up to me and Kate to say good-bye. "I wish I had more time," she said, and we watched as she took off her satin high heels and exchanged them for sneakers. "I just wanted to say I love you both. I haven't found such good friends anywhere. I'm not drunk, I really mean all this . . ." And she pressed her hand to her heart, then hugged each of us before she ran off to find Dan. In a short while, they were walking arm in arm to their battered blue VW van, as everyone cheered and blew soap bubbles at them. Sylvia threw her bouquet out the window and Dan honked the van's horn all the way down the street, and then our lovely friends were gone.

"Anne, do you remember that night when we were at Sylvia's and sketched each other?" Kate asked.

"Of course," I said. I remembered it clearly. Sylvia had made a sketch of my face floating in a sea of black, my eyes closed, as if I were dreaming. At one point, she had stared at me, and said, "I see now. You're entirely in your head, aren't you?" I was a little taken aback and didn't know whether to be pleased or wounded. It was a dissection as well as a caress, and it was like this as we sketched, our hands moving over paper as we followed the hills and shadows of each other's faces.

"I still have some of our sketches pinned on my wall," Kate said. "It makes me think it isn't hopeless after all, that at least somewhere in the world people see me as I want to be seen." She began to cry because no matter how many gypsy women tell her to act with her head, Kate will always wear her heart on her sleeve. I took her wrist and shook it gently.

II. Dream Lounge

Vincent always seemed so contemplative, sitting on my porch in the early morning, smoking his first cigarette of the day and drinking black coffee. He held the cigarette slanted between his fingers, his right hand resting on his lap, and I liked to watch him flick off the ash and bring the cigarette to his lips. Where we lived in upstate New York, it was winter six months of the year and there was snow on the ground until April. We sat on the porch wearing our winter coats, mugs of steaming coffee resting on our armchairs, our breath turning into vapor. Vincent had a perfect memory and recited verses to me:

> *Thaw follows frost; hard on the heel of spring*
> *Treads summer sure to die, for hard on hers*
> *Comes autumn with his apples scattering;*
> *Then back to wintertide, when nothing stirs.*

It seemed as if the snow would never melt under a sky so white, and when I walked along the salted streets in town, warm air unfurling from my mouth, I felt the hopelessness of the season, as if I were suspended in a dream.

Vincent thought I was an innocent. He said he could tell just by looking at me. Sometimes, though, when he drank himself into a stupor and I held his arm to keep him from falling on the sidewalk, I thought he was the naïve one. Of course, his vulnerability appealed to me. When we made love, he sometimes left bruises on my breasts, and afterward, I felt oddly pleased looking at myself in the mirror. For once in my life, I didn't recognize myself, and I was sorry when the colors faded and there was nothing but blank skin as before.

I had been hired to teach English for a year at an elite boarding school in the Adirondacks. The closest city was two hours away, and many of the young single teachers usually wound up at the local inn on Friday night for drinks. This is how I met Vincent. He came up to our table with one hand in his pocket, the other holding a martini, looking very dapper in his light brown suit and gold tie. I would later discover that he was popular with his students, who liked to call him Gatsby. Vincent had a loose grin on his face, and I envied him immediately. He seemed more at ease than any of us in that room. He sat down next to me, and I found out that he taught Philosophy.

"So who do you prefer? Plato or Nietzsche?" I asked him.

"I like both, actually. I'm amphibian in that way."

Caitlin, a teacher who, like me, had just moved here several weeks before, was asking everyone at the table what there was to do in this town. She had already tried the two pizza places and the execrable Chinese restaurant, and during her first week in town she had broken down and gone to the movie theater and watched an inane film about sexually attractive clones. "But the really creepy thing was that slide show before the movie started," she said, and everyone else at the table burst out laughing. "You haven't seen it?" she asked me. "Before the movie starts, they project all these happy snapshots of people in town. I'd been here only a few days, remember, but I recognized half the people smiling in the photographs. It was terrifying."

"Well, I don't know if this will interest you, Caitlin," Vincent said, "but Richard Goode will be performing in the chapel next month."

"Who is Richard Goode?" she asked.

"He's a pianist. One of the best."

The conversation drifted, and I turned to Vincent and asked if he played the piano.

"Only left-hand pieces," he said. I thought at first he was being whimsical until I glanced down at his hands. His right hand rested in his lap, the index finger pointing stiffly out and the other fingers curled painfully under. "Oh, that one isn't worth looking at," he said, and he put it back into his pocket. "Now, I do like my left hand. I think it's my best feature." He showed it to me. It was a fine hand, the hand of a pianist, with long, sensitive fingers and short, broad nails.

"A beautiful hand," I agreed.

"Why, thank you," he said, studying it in a fond, careless way. Then he looked down at his glass, which was empty except for an olive dangling on a toothpick. The waitress came by and asked if he wanted another martini.

"Please."

"Bombay Sapphire, right?"

"With three olives."

His hazel eyes, with their flecks of gold, were bemused yet curiously inert. I should have stood up then and wished him good night. He probably had no other thought than to retreat further into his haze, and I knew it was foolish to follow a person in search of his own pleasure.

He gazed at me for a moment as if I reminded him of someone. "There is a needle poking me in this chair," he said gravely.

"There is? Where?"

He took my hand and guided it to the spot. Beneath the blue fabric, I felt something sharp against my finger. He let go of my wrist and smiled at me. Later he would confess that he had pointed out the needle in order to touch my hand.

He invited me to his place to play the piano, and as we

walked to his apartment, I felt exactly as I did when I was a child and had to perform in front of a group of strangers. My hands were icy cold, and my chest felt tight and hollow. During my last piano recital, when I was thirteen years old, I had frozen in the middle of a piece, unable to remember what came next. There was a terrible breathless silence in the audience as I stared at my hands resting lightly on the keys, and I felt far away but also at the very center of things, as if I were attending my own funeral. I started the piece over from the very beginning, but this time an automaton was playing. Everyone clapped in relief when I finished. I stood up and looked out over the audience and saw my piano teacher covering her face with her hands. She had known me since I was six years old, and at the beginning of my first lesson she had made me take off every single one of the bright tinsel rings I had worn for her.

Vincent lived above a florist shop in a redbrick walk-up. His apartment was elegant in an impersonal way, as though he were a boarder living in already furnished rooms. I would find out later that his antique cherry furniture had been handed down to him from an aunt in Charleston, its genteel character sullied by piles of paper, coffee mugs, empty beer bottles, and saucers turned into ashtrays. Above the mantelpiece, he had hung his diplomas, and most of his books were depressing leather-bound editions with gold lettering on the spines, glossy little caskets I would hesitate before opening. In the dim light, his piano crouched like a dark, sleek animal in the corner.

I sank into an orange parlor chair and listened to him play a waltz by Brahms. My sister and I had played the same piece as a duet, but we had played it as if a relentless metronome were ticking inside our heads. Vincent played the piece with leisurely grace, a spaciousness between the notes which suggested a longing for something else. He followed the Brahms with a more difficult piece by Scriabin, and though he played well I noticed gaps in the music where his one hand could not accomplish the work of two. The music was more poignant to me for this reason, but I knew it would offend him if I ever said so.

"Don't you want to play?" he asked when he had finished.

"I'm not very good."

"Does that matter?"

"I get more pleasure listening to you play."

He smiled at my cowardice. When I wrapped my arms tight around myself, he asked if I was cold.

"No, I'm fine," I said.

"Are you sure?" He got up and closed the window. "Why don't we play something together?"

I sat beside him on the bench, and Vincent suggested we try the Gladiolus Rag. I thought it would be easier to play the part for the left hand, but I kept hitting the wrong notes. Vincent played the melody with beautiful ease, and I felt bad that he had to suffer me as his duet partner. Finally, I gave up and took my hand off the keyboard. "It's too painful to listen," I said.

"You are very hard on yourself, aren't you?" he asked, and he began to kiss me gently around my lips, small chaste kisses that surprised me. For some reason he made me think of a giraffe the way he kissed me with his mouth closed. His innocent grazing was oddly touching. We kissed some more, and I asked if we could move to his bedroom.

"Are you sure?" Vincent asked. "You want to go so fast?"

"Oh, it doesn't matter."

He looked hurt by this answer.

"I mean I don't care if we rush things," I said, and he gave me a lopsided grin.

I stayed over at Vincent's that night. At about two in the

morning, I woke up to hear him talking in his sleep. The room was shrouded in darkness, and I thought at first the voice was emanating from a corner of my mind. I struggled to remember where I was beside this dreaming shape who spoke so reasonably about blue caviar and the hinterland. The more lucid I was, the less I understood. Vincent's words fell upon my ears like music, then dropped into oblivion. A part of me was tempted to get up and write down everything he said, to discover his secret thoughts, the desires he hid even from himself. Who doesn't wish to know the very heart of a person? But I was too lazy to stir from bed and preferred to drowse in the warm dark beside him. I tried to commit the stream of words to memory before falling asleep, but in the morning his sentences had disappeared along with my dreams.

In early November, after the first snow had fallen, we went to hear Richard Goode perform in the chapel. Vincent suggested that we sit on the side balcony, where we could have a view of the pianist's hands. He was appalled by the empty pews. In the city, Richard Goode's concerts sold out regularly, but here in the village bounded by mountains and snow, hardly anyone had come. I didn't mind the half-empty chapel. It seemed more intimate, and as Goode played a Beethoven sonata, I looked out over the audience, my attention drawn toward the high windows, the music filling the empty space of the chapel. I listened, and it sounded as if the heart were asking for something in a delicate way, making little excursions, taking desultory paths around the question, but what it wanted was something so small and particular, and always it kept returning to the same note, bittersweet and piercing. I could hear Vincent breathing as he sat close to me, our legs barely touching, and when he leaned forward with bowed head, I wanted to kiss the nape of his neck.

I remembered how as a young girl I had restlessly wandered the woods behind my house. I had read books—Lucy opening the wardrobe, Alice falling through a rabbit hole—and felt the ordinariness of my life. Branches swayed, lifting and dropping tremendously, and I made myself dizzy looking up at them. I waited, but another world did not open. I grew older. I moved to different cities. I read and dreamed and looked out of windows. My hands and feet were always cold. I began to feel like a brittle doll sitting upright in a tiny chair. I wanted to be picked up and thrown out the window or smashed against a wall. If I were shattered and put back together again, I would be able to look any person fully in the eye.

When we first started seeing each other, Vincent asked me a lot of embarrassing questions. He wanted to know about all the odd places where I'd had sex and then volunteered some stories of his own. One involved a dinner party. Between the main course and dessert, he and his date had separately excused themselves from the table and then met up in their host's bedroom. "It was rude of us," he admitted. "Everyone knew what was going on." He then asked me if I'd ever done anything like that, and I told him I hadn't.

He also asked me what I liked in bed. When he saw me hesitate, he said, "It's true that you have to be careful revealing your fantasies to someone. When you each know what pleases the other, then sooner or later it begins to feel scripted." He was finally able to get it out of me that I wanted him to be forceful. "I like the idea of someone feeling strong desire for me," I said. "I want to feel overwhelmed."

"A rape fantasy," he said.

"Hmm. I guess you could call it that."

As for Vincent, he liked women's calves. He had purchased videos of women in short airy dresses and high heels walking slowly up stairs or stepping down the street and turning around with care.

When we had sex now, Vincent was rougher with me. "I wasn't sure I'd like it, but I'm really getting into this," he told me. He pulled my hair and bit my cheeks and put his hand over my mouth as if he were trying to suffocate me. Sometimes it felt silly. And sometimes I bit and bruised him in return. A few times Vincent went too far, and I felt myself shrinking away from him. All the while, I felt we were getting closer.

He once asked me why I was attracted to him. And I told him it was because he did things I'd never do. It was easy for him to cross boundaries, whereas I could never be so reckless. He reflected for a moment, then said, "You say this, but really I'm just a tweedy, bookish person who teaches high school kids."

Going to Amsterdam over spring break was Vincent's idea. He had been there twice already. The first time he hooked up with his friend Anton, which surprised him, as he'd never been with another man. The second time he brought Lisa, the violinist with the shapely calves who later broke his heart when she dropped him for an older man. When I asked, Vincent said the trip with Lisa had been disappointing. She was too uptight. "A librarian type," he said, smiling. "Just like you."

In Amsterdam, the black narrow houses along the canal looked like dollhouses tilting against the sky. I didn't have to be on drugs to find the city unreal. The dark rows of old-fashioned bicycles, the bare trees and solitary lampposts, the green boats, the murky, glimmering water wherever we walked.

We smoked White Widow and ate space cake, sucking on sugar cubes and drinking black coffee. We entered a store called Dream Lounge, and as Vincent looked at mushrooms beneath a glass case, I walked around the room, trying to pretend the floor wasn't moving. It kept rising and falling beneath me. For a while, I stared at a sleek sculpture of a cat sitting on the counter. It had the menacing beauty of something alive, its body slippery and fine, the very pattern of its coat transcendent. The cat gazed at me with its round gold eyes, and I thought it was a presence from another world until it yawned. I stroked its head, and the cat purred automatically like a motor, but I knew it was afraid of me.

Outside, I held on to Vincent's arm, but this was like holding on to a stick in the middle of the ocean. Neither of us knew where we were going. Vincent had retreated into a numb insensibility, his steps heavy and flat, and I had lost my mind or whatever it was that had separated me from the world. A person could lead me anywhere in the city, and I would be unable to say no. We circled and passed the same storefronts like zombies, and I felt a rising hopelessness as I put one foot in front of the other.

We gave up finally and went into a McDonald's. "I need to sit down," Vincent said. "Could you get me a cheeseburger?" He stumbled off to a booth and left me squinting under the bright lights. The man ahead of me in line kept turning around to stare at me. He knew I was sunk deep in some underwater reality. I stepped up to the counter, but I wasn't sure I'd be able to speak. "One cheeseburger," I said carefully, and the cashier frowned. All the registers began to beep and flash — I was sure I had set them off — and the cashier informed me that they would deliver the cheeseburger to my seat.

Vincent was slumped in a booth, his palms splayed out at his sides. He looked at me as I sat down and asked where the cheeseburger was.

"They're bringing it to us," I whispered.

"What?"

I shook my head, afraid the man in the next booth was listening.

"You aren't going to talk?" Vincent asked.

I shut my eyes, smiling slightly. This was a nightmare. I wanted to be back in our hotel room. The cheeseburger arrived, and I kept one hand over my face as I watched Vincent eat.

"You're acting very weird," he told me. Then he began to sing: "*Pa*-ra-*noi*-a! Para-*noi*-a! Para-*noi*-a!"

I got up from the booth and waited for Vincent outside. He seemed to take a long time finishing his cheeseburger. Everyone was looking at him as he attempted to throw away the wrapper on his tray.

And then we were walking again through that unreal city of thin slanting houses and gray water. Amsterdam opened before us like an empty museum, drawing us into its ever expanding ring of canals, a picturesque labyrinth of narrow streets and bridges, and all the while I couldn't shake the presentiment that at the next corner something terrible awaited us. I pressed Vincent's arm. Didn't he see? We were separated from the world by only a fragile layer of skin. Our bodies were bubbles waiting to burst!

"Is that so?" Vincent said.

I wanted to go back to the hotel.

"What are you hoping to find there?" Vincent asked.

Peace and comfort. A place to hide.

"That would be nice," Vincent said. He took the map out of his pocket and peered at it, then stuffed it back into his coat. "Hopeless," he muttered. "I can't make any sense of it."

I squeezed his arm, and Vincent took the map out again and moved to the side of a building where there was more light.

People walked by and looked at us. They knew we were lost and regarded us with contempt.

"Our hotel is this way," Vincent said. We walked several blocks before he realized the numbers were going in the wrong direction. We turned around, and I was afraid to look up at the houses. "Just a few more blocks, I promise," Vincent said, but I didn't believe him.

And yet here was our hotel, and we were going through the revolving doors. I hurried past the receptionist, trying to still my face. She knew, of course, she must see this thing all the time. Oh, to get to our ugly little room, what a relief that would be, and I told the elevator to hurry, please hurry! Down the sober carpeted hallway and then Vincent fiddling with the door until it sprang open and I collapsed into a heap on the bed. Vincent stood in front of the mirror, trying to get out of his shirt, but his arms had gotten stuck somehow. "I can't seem to take off my shirt," Vincent said, and we looked at each other and burst into laughter. I rolled onto my stomach, and Vincent doubled over and fell to the floor, where he lay with his eyes closed.

"Do you think we're being too loud?" I asked after a moment.

"Not at all," he replied.

I crawled off the bed and rested my head on his chest, and his fingers stirred my hair gently. "You should just give in," he said. "That's why you suffer. You're fighting it when you should just let go."

"Just let go," I said. "You make it sound so easy. But you might as well tell me to just let go and jump in front of a train. Just let go and throw myself off a cliff. I can't help it if I have an instinct to preserve myself."

Vincent bugged his eyes and bared his teeth at me, and I let out a cry and covered my eyes. I had a sudden creeping sensation that the warm body I lay against was a stranger's.

"Come on," he said. "You can open your eyes."

I shook my head. I wanted to get away from him, but I was too scared to move.

"I promise I won't make that face again."

"You do?"

"Yes."

I opened my eyes, and he leered at me, showing his crooked bottom teeth. "You aren't to be trusted," I said, pressing my hands over my face. I felt my heart racing.

He chuckled. "Just because you're paranoid doesn't mean they're not coming to get you."

I heard a rustling sound close by but didn't move. I knew he was trying to trick me, to scare me into opening my eyes. What was that sound? Like plastic crinkling. I imagined him smothering me with a plastic bag.

"I guess this means you're not going to sleep with me tonight?"

Ha! That was the last thing I wanted.

He made as if to get up. "Well, I can go away then."

"No, don't go," I said, lifting my head and gazing at him. I wanted to trust him, but people changed so quickly, and then it was as if you never knew them at all.

"Don't look at me like that," he said.

"Why not?"

"I don't like it." He put his arm over his eyes. "Stop looking at me."

I smiled. "But why?"

"I don't want to be examined like I'm some kind of specimen."

"But you're such an interesting one."

"I knew it. You're nothing but a voyeur," he said. "If I were dying, all you would do is look on."

I blinked. "It seems I'm not the only one who is paranoid." I pushed myself off his chest and got into bed, covering my head with a blanket.

In the middle of the night I woke up and heard voices in the hallway. It was a low murmuring that I wanted, but failed, to understand. I imagined neighbors congregating outside our door, whispering about us. Any moment they would knock loudly and burst in. I closed my eyes but couldn't stop the darkness from swelling inside me. An imperceptible crack had opened along my skull, and through this tiny hairline fracture, shadows seeped in to stroke and deform my thoughts. There could be no relief, no place to hide. I pressed my hands over my eyes, watching my thoughts darken and twist.

In the morning, I woke up and saw a pearl gray light emanating from the edge of the curtains, felt the cool, clean sheets and the bland stillness of the furniture around me, and I knew immediately. My thoughts were clear, and I was in my right mind. I wanted to wake Vincent up to tell him, but instead I quickly dressed and left the room to take a walk.

Outside, the air was crisp, the sky a delicate blue, and I felt the bright calm of the morning. A man on a bicycle passed by, reading a newspaper. I crossed over a bridge, looking at the bare trees and lilac brick houses reflected in the water, and then I stopped at a bakery, where I bought a chocolate croissant and a lovely round apple cake. I found some steps to sit on and devoured both. You could never find such good pastries in America, so delicious and beautiful, and inexpensive, too. The woman at the bakery had treated me with just the right courtesy, neither too warm or too cold, and I liked her sensible air, the neat green dress she wore, her shining coiled hair.

Surrounding her were all the things she had made so perfectly that it was almost a shame to eat them. I returned and bought an apple cake for Vincent before I walked back to the hotel.

Vincent frowned when I told him I had never appreciated my sanity before. I was going to remain delightfully sane for the rest of the trip. He could do as he pleased, but I wanted my mind to be clear.

"You're overreacting," he said. "Last night wasn't so bad."

"What are you talking about? It was a nightmare."

"But don't you think it's funny we ended up in a McDonald's?"

"It's funny *now.*"

"But remember how we laughed when we got back to the hotel room?"

"Yes. But the rest was a nightmare."

"I was afraid you'd react like this," he said, and he got up to take a shower.

For the rest of the trip, I watched Vincent get high, and I suppose what he said about me was true. I had the curiosity and coldness to look on. I shepherded him about, giving him my arm, and he walked slowly and stiffly by my side like an old man. He told me about the luminous things he saw, how pale umbrellas glowed like jellyfish and pink flowers vibrated on a woman's dress. But mostly he was silent, a tall, morose figure in his black coat, the sleeve on one side dangling lower than the other. When confronted with his own image in the mirror, he refused to look. What he wanted was to distort his senses, to numb himself from reality and keep it at bay, and I felt a loneliness watching him. What if life were to catch up with him and not let him go? At night, as we lay curled together, his arm around my waist, I placed his left hand against my breast and held it there until I fell asleep.

We returned to New York, and there were small depressions in the snow, a faint glistening as it melted and revealed islands of green. I thought spring had finally arrived. But it snowed again, and it seemed like perfect winter landscape, everything covered in whiteness. Snow, like sleep, could make you oblivious to anything.

Vincent broke up with me in June. At the end of July, I was driving to school one last time to clean out my classroom when I saw Vincent's car a block ahead of mine. I turned down another street and waited silently by the side of the road until enough time had passed, and then I drove on to the parking lot and found him waiting for me.

"Well, hello," he said, smiling. "I have some good news."

"Oh, yes?" I said brightly. "What is it?"

He told me that he had quit smoking. "My doctor said I would die of a heart attack by the time I was forty if I didn't stop."

"But what about all those cigarettes I gave you?"

"They're still sitting on my dresser, but I haven't touched them. I haven't had a drink either. It's too tempting to smoke if I have a drink."

"How dramatic," I said.

"It's not really dramatic."

"I mean, all these life changes you're making." I couldn't help but sound a little bitter. I looked down and saw his bare feet in sandals. I had never seen him wear sandals before, and the sight of his pale, bloated feet with a dull bluish cast to them repulsed me, and I was very glad for this feeling. "So do you suffer much?" I asked. "Is it true that you become a more boring person if you stop smoking?"

"Every hour, I have a craving," he said.

"You should give me your cigarettes if they tempt you."

"They don't tempt me."

"Well, give them to me anyway," I said. "Maybe I'll start smoking." But even as I said this, I knew it wasn't true. I would never become a smoker.

We walked slowly toward the building, and I sensed that he wanted to continue talking to me just as I wanted to continue talking to him. He told me that he had gone canoeing on the lake by himself one afternoon, that he had taken to swimming laps in the pool, and I imagined him doing these things, living a more austere and reflective life of solitary, quiet pleasures. The reformed individual, the hedonist turned ascetic, living moderately and no longer indulging in sensation. And then it struck me that he was probably doing all this exercise to make himself attractive for a younger woman.

"So how are you doing?" he asked me.

"I'm doing fine," I said. That wasn't true. I wasn't eating and wanted to disappear. But instead of turning as light as a ghost, my flesh felt tired and heavy, and I dragged myself from one room to another, unable to sleep. The doctor had prescribed some sleeping pills (I had lied to him and said I had jet lag), but they knocked me out for only four hours before I woke up again. Awake or asleep, I felt empty, but I would be fine soon enough. That was the sad thing.

Vincent folded his arms around me, and I felt awkward, ready to spring away, but he only pressed me closer. It confused me because for the moment at least it seemed that he cared for me, that he was the one who was more true. My hand slid down his arm until I reached the edge of his hand, and I held his last two fingers softly before letting go.

III. Lilies

I moved to San Francisco and soon met my businessman, the one etched on my palm whom I was supposed to marry.

I taught English at a private Christian school, where the principal informed me I would be fired if anyone saw me buying alcohol. I began to drink a glass of wine by myself at dinnertime anyway, always choosing white because I wanted to have a taste in my mouth that was simple and light and clear. I read Buddhist books about impermanence, how there is no self or soul connecting the pieces of ourselves together, and I liked the idea of relinquishing my ego and merging with the void and of having no more desires for anything or anyone.

Vincent and I were still in touch. We exchanged polite, impersonal e-mails a few times each month, and any small detail he was willing to give me about his life made me brood about him a little more.

He once told me, with some regret, that he was an amoral person. I had been fascinated and disturbed by the number of women he had slept with, all those bodies he had left behind. Now he had left me behind, and it was sobering to realize that there was nothing that distinguished me from the rest.

I met the businessman at a dinner party hosted by a friend. He was holding a drink the color of avocados with a marigold floating on top. "What's that?" I asked. "It's very pretty."

"Pea soup. Do you want to try?" He handed me his glass, and I took a sip. "Well?"

I hesitated. "It tastes like . . ."

"Pea soup?"

"Perhaps if you put in some salt."

"Hmm. I don't ever taste what I cook before serving it."

"You made this?"

"Well, it isn't any good."

"It's quite aesthetic. The flower is a nice touch."

He shrugged. "I always care more about how the food looks than how it tastes." The businessman was tall and thickening around the middle. He had a heavy, handsome face that was at once masculine and babyish, light quick eyes, and a cleft chin. I already knew from my friend, who wanted to set us up, that his name was Clay and that he was from Georgia. He liked old films and owned a small collection of Venetian masks.

Clay asked me what I did on the weekends, and I told him I went to concerts at Davies Symphony Hall, where I paid twenty dollars for a Center Terrace seat overlooking the back of the orchestra.

"You go alone?" he asked.

I blushed and asked if he had heard of Leon Fleisher, who was performing next week. "He's this pianist who was at the height of his career when he was afflicted with a neurological disorder," I said. "It made the muscles of his right hand contract and his fingers curl under. For a while, he couldn't perform in concerts, but then he developed a repertoire of left-hand pieces. There's a surprising amount of pieces you can play for the left hand alone."

Clay smiled. "You want to pay to go see someone play with one hand?"

This made me like him a little less. "Well, he's still brilliant," I said. "I mean he plays better with one hand than most people play with two. But the thing is, he recently regained the use of his right hand. He gets injections that relax the muscles, so now he can play with both hands."

"But he can play only the easy pieces, right?" He smiled at me and said he was only teasing. "Let's go hear this Leon Fleisher guy together."

I hesitated for a moment. "All right," I said.

I didn't tell Clay I got a painful pleasure out of going to these concerts by myself. The only reason I knew about Leon Fleisher was because of Vincent, of course. His interests and tastes exerted a more powerful influence over me now that he was no longer in my life.

The following week, Clay and I watched Leon Fleisher appear onstage, looking battered and untamed in spite of his tuxedo. Set apart and shielded from the world by square black glasses, he was a sturdy, deep-chested man with spindly legs, his hair streaked black and iron gray, his Mephistophelian beard whitening at the chin. He was larger than life and yet also all too human. There was the frailty of his age, the remarkable history of his hands. He played a Mozart concerto with lightness and joy, and as I leaned forward in my chair, I was startled when Clay reached over and patted my back. A moment later, he removed his hand and began flipping through his program and reading the concert notes.

During the intermission, he held out my jacket for me as I slipped it on, and we walked onto the terrace and leaned over the railing, looking across the street at the lighted dome of City Hall. "Sometimes my attention wanders when I listen to music," Clay told me. "I'm bored, and I think about other things. But it's funny how it can get under your skin when you're least expecting it. When it stirs you up, there's nothing you can do. Seriously, there were moments just now when I felt I was going to lose it." He grinned, putting a knuckle to the corner of his eye, and I smiled as well.

"A sensitive businessman," I said.

"Whatever preconceptions you have about me are dead wrong," he replied.

We walked back through the shining lobby with its walls of glass, past people sitting at small tables and others standing in line at the bar, couples sipping their drinks and looking out at the city or leaning back against the windows and observing other people go by. The constant murmur of voices, the sound of laughter and tinkling glasses, filled my ears. Rising beneath this din, the whirling cacophony of the orchestra as musicians practiced or tuned their instruments, a chaos of sound that lent itself to anticipation.

Clay guided me through the crowd by touching my elbow, and it occurred to me that anyone who saw us might think we were together and in love. We found our seats again, and as the concert resumed I felt disappointed by my own detachment. This evening with Clay was pleasant enough, but there was no part of me that was deeply engaged. I glanced at my watch, then looked out into the audience at the sea of cold, pensive faces, the fine glittering dresses of the women, the sober husbands crumpled in their chairs.

Clay called me a few days later and said he wanted to take me out to dinner that night. "I'm going away this weekend and want to see you before I leave."

"Why don't we do something when you get back?"

"No, I'm sorry," he said, "but you'll have to give me a compelling reason why you can't go out to dinner with me tonight."

I thought this was unusual. Here was a definite man who made demands of me. And so I agreed to meet him for dinner.

At the restaurant, Clay said he had been looking forward to

seeing me all day. I opened my menu, but a fog had descended on my brain and I couldn't make up my mind. Clay merely glanced at the menu and closed it, observing my confusion with a smile on his lips.

"You're a decisive person," I said.

"I was born knowing what I want." He spoke with charming ease and a subtle drawl that disarmed me.

The appetizer arrived, figs wrapped in prosciutto, and I cut my fig carefully in half before taking a small bite. "The way you're eating sums up the differences between us," he said, popping an entire fig into his mouth.

The restaurant was small and crowded, and we had to raise our voices to hear each other. Finally, he set down his fork and leaned forward with his hands folded together. "I'm not going to try to talk over this noise," he said. "I just want to look at you." He cocked his head and gazed at me, at one point blinking rapidly as if he were starry-eyed. I tried to stare back at him boldly, but I lacked the nerve and looked down at my plate. I was playing the typical role of a woman who is looked at, and it made me very unhappy.

"Look," I said. "If you're not going to talk to me, then I don't want to get coffee with you afterward."

This put his gazing to an end, and he paid for the meal, one that I couldn't have afforded. Outside the restaurant, he said, "You greeted me so coldly before. Can I have a perfunctory hug now?"

"Of course." I opened my arms, and he pressed me fully against him. When I tried to back away, he wouldn't let go and squeezed me even tighter. It was unpleasant to be so close, to feel his desire when I felt nothing at all. At last, Clay released me, and we walked on to the café. I tried to pay for the coffee, but he looked at me in a steely way, as if I had just insulted him. "Money is no object," he said lightly, taking out his wallet.

Later, as he walked me back to my car, he insisted on walking on my left-hand side, closer to the curb. "Why that side?" I asked.

"If a car should lose control, I'll be able to push you away in time and sacrifice myself."

"Well, *thanks*," I said. We had arrived at my car, but he continued to hover beside me. I was nervous and afraid that he would ask for a perfunctory kiss. "Well, bye now."

"Hey, I'm sorry I've been so pushy," he said, moving toward me. His stubble grazed my face, and I felt his moist parted lips, the warm insistence of his breath, as he kissed me on the cheek.

A few days later I received a bouquet of oriental lilies. Only three lilies had bloomed, and it seemed a modest arrangement at first. I knew I should call to thank him, but I felt an obscure dread that manifested itself as passivity, and I couldn't do it. He called me later that evening and told me the flowers were a small gift.

The lilies smelled heavy and sweet and close. Each day another bud opened, and the bouquet spread out and grew more lush until I counted nine starlike, poisonous faces the size of my palm. They crowded my desk, blocking my peaceful view of the bay. If I drew the blinds, I came away with flecks of pollen on my sleeve, and even when I was careful not to brush against the anthers, the slightest stir or exhalation was enough for them to mark me.

I once asked Vincent if he had ever slept with someone he wasn't attracted to. He had widened his eyes and with careful emphasis, because he knew what he was going to say would upset me, he confessed that he had been with Miranda, one of the teachers at our school. "People say you can have sex only with those you love," he told me, "but you can have sex with those you don't even like."

When Clay called me again, I didn't pick up the phone. He called two more times after that and left messages, and I wondered why a person became less desirable when they showed need. His interest in me seemed odd, even unnatural. I had done little to encourage him, yet he continued to press on. I recalled the moment when Clay took his shoes off in the café and put his socked feet on the bench beside me. It was an intimacy I hadn't asked for, but he remained oblivious of my feelings, quite comfortable in fact with his feet lying there next to me. He was so sure of himself, acting as if he knew something I didn't, and I felt an irrational fear that the gypsy woman had cursed me. I saw myself moving toward him in fits and starts, a dangling, convulsive puppet.

For some reason, Clay was fixated on me just as I was fixated on Vincent. Vincent was probably fixated on a former student of his, a twenty-year-old blonde with cornflower blue eyes, a pointy nose, and a pale little smile. When he and I were still together, I had stopped by Vincent's apartment one afternoon without warning and found him and the girl playing cards together at his dining room table. The girl was slouched in a chair with a languid expression on her face, her long legs slanting under the table. Vincent sat upright, his feet spread slightly apart, slowly flipping over cards. Their legs were close enough to be touching, and an image of the two spending the entire afternoon in bed with their legs entwined and then playing this desultory game of cards rose up before me. The girl immediately straightened up in her chair when she saw me.

"Anne," Vincent said without missing a beat, "this is Lisa. I'm helping her procrastinate from writing her final paper."

I already knew who she was. Vincent had told me he wanted to sleep with her when she was his student. I felt unbearably hot all at once, standing there in the middle of the room, and I realized that as usual I was wearing too many clothes, whereas the girl was dressed in a tank top and a short skirt, things that you're supposed to wear when you're young. I took off my jacket, but it was hard for me to focus and reply to what Vincent was saying. I finally gave up trying. "Well, I'll leave you two alone now," I said, turning to leave.

"Bye," the girl said quietly—it was almost a whisper—and I quickly left.

Vincent called me a half hour later at my house. "Why did you leave like that?" he asked me. "It was so sad the way you rushed out. You were practically running away from us. Lisa felt awful and left early."

"I'm glad," I told him.

"Oh, you are, are you?"

"You're sleeping with her, aren't you? You've always said you're amoral, the type to cheat, so just tell me the truth, you fucking degenerate. Are you sleeping with her?"

"You know, in a way, I'm flattered by your reaction," Vincent said. "Your jealousy makes me think you really care about me. But it also makes me like you a little less. You're so quick to think the worst of me."

I never knew for sure whether Vincent cheated on me. What was certain was that he liked me less after that. By the time we broke up, he said he felt nothing. He didn't want to pretend anymore and dreaded having to touch me.

In the evenings, I prepared lesson plans and graded student papers in a large open café in my neighborhood. One night, I looked across the room and saw a man with a small wrinkled face staring at me. He had a clipboard tilted toward him and seemed to be drawing something, and the way he looked at me, moving his pencil across the page, filled me with alarm: I thought he might be sketching me. We made eye contact, he smiled, and I quickly looked down. The woman at the table beside me got up to leave, and I was dismayed to see the man gather up his clipboard and stainless steel mug and approach me. For the first time, I noticed he was missing his entire left arm. He set his things down at the empty table beside mine, then went back to the other table to retrieve his satchel and long walking stick. As his back was turned, I took the opportunity to glance at his clipboard.

The drawing was crude and nonsensical, done with colored pencils. It depicted a man standing behind an electric pole. What the man was doing behind that pole was a mystery, but I suspected it was fairly obscene. The electric pole rose in front of him in a grand phallic statement.

The one-armed man returned, eyeing me as he sat down. He was wearing a beret and sandals, with one gold stud in his ear. He examined his drawing and began coloring with itty-bitty strokes, sometimes dabbing at them with an eraser, turning the clipboard this way and that to judge what he had done. Now and then he grunted or made small exclamations over his work, then turned to look at me slyly as if to include me in his private conversation. I tried to ignore him, but I couldn't focus on what I was doing. Finally, I crossed my arms and glared at the television mounted in the corner. There was a baseball game on.

"Do you know what the score is?" he asked me.

"No idea," I said. I picked up my crumpled napkin and brushed at my computer screen, and the one-armed man got up out of his seat and returned with a few napkins in his hand.

"You'll want some clean ones for that," he said, presenting them to me. "I saw you typing and thought to myself, Wow, she can really type." He smiled, peering at my screen. "So what is it you were typing?"

"I'm trying to do some work."

"Too busy to talk to me, huh? Hey, what's that doing there?" He leaned over, his finger touching a bruise on my arm.

I got up and stuffed my papers into my bag, picked up my laptop, and headed toward a table at the opposite end of the café.

"So you want to play musical chairs?" he called out behind me.

I settled into my new space but was too distracted to do any work now. Even from across the café, I could feel his presence demanding my attention, and when I glanced over in his direction, he was staring right at me, his mouth moving, though I couldn't hear a word he was saying.

In my studio, I stared at the lilies from Clay. A few had darkened to a moribund purple, the glossy petals curling back, starting to fall in clumps on my desk.

On Sunday afternoon I was startled by an imperious rapping at my door. It was Clay, looking as though he'd just stepped off the golf course. He handed me a box of chocolates. "Sorry to disturb you," he said, smiling. "But I've been forced to take action. You haven't been returning my calls."

"No," I said. "I've been busy."

"Doing what exactly?"

I shrugged but didn't answer.

He stepped closer, pretending to peer around me. "So are you going to invite me in? I want to see your digs."

I hesitated. "Well, I'm working now."

"I won't take up too much time."

I opened the door wider for him. "There's really not much to see." Besides the tiny kitchen, there was only one room with a chair in the corner, my desk facing the window, and my unmade bed with its heap of blankets. "It's cozy," he said, sitting in the chair.

I sat down on a corner of my bed. "Thanks for these," I said, opening the box of chocolates. "Do you want one?"

He shook his head, gazing at me. "You should wear your hair down."

"I do," I said. "Today, though, I'm wearing it up."

"I don't like reserved women," he said. "Shy is okay, but not reserved. Now, my question is are you being shy or reserved?"

I looked at him, feeling a fascination but also a repulsion, as with the lilies he had given me. "I'm being reserved."

"Well, maybe we can change that." He got up and sat down beside me. "Does this make you feel uncomfortable?" He smiled, staring me down, and I couldn't help it and looked away. I wondered what it would be like to be so confident, to never show doubt, to insist, to bombard, to never hesitate or relent. I was sick and afraid of such people.

"Why aren't you looking at me?" he asked. "Are you being shy now?" He reached out to turn my face toward him, but I shoved his hand away. His brow furrowed as he leaned in closer, and I jabbed him with my elbow, getting quickly off the bed. "You need to back off," I said.

He stood up quickly as well. "I was just about to do that," he said. There was a red spot on his cheek, and I could hear him breathing through his mouth.

"I mean, what were you doing just now? You can't force me to like you. I don't like you and never will."

He nodded curtly. "Message taken loud and clear."

"If a person doesn't return your calls, it means they're not interested."

He was silent, reflecting. "I'm not usually this aggressive," he said.

"I find that hard to believe."

"No, really. I'm usually a more diffident kind of guy, but I've been trying to change that."

There was something slightly pitiful about this, which dismayed me. It opened up the whole possibility that the businessman was someone I would have to feel sorry for. "Diffidence is a good thing," I said.

He smiled. "Well, I'll go now."

I nodded. "So long, Clay."

In December, Richard Goode gave a concert in San Francisco. More than a year had passed since the concert in the chapel, and I sat by myself on the second tier, barely able to make out the tiny faraway figure that was Richard Goode on the stage. Between each piece, people coughed violently, an unrestrained hacking that spread through the auditorium as they relieved the itches in their throats. A ripple of laughter arose at these desperate sounds while Richard Goode sat on the bench and mopped his brow with a handkerchief, which he stuffed back into his pocket. We wanted so much from him, to be transported, to go deeper into our memories, to lose ourselves in the feeling that the music evoked in us, to wander around for a while in our dreams, but we could not escape the minor irritations of reality, our own bodily complaints, and the distraction of other bodies surrounding us—people in the audience sneezing or whispering or looking at their cell phones or clandestinely untwisting a candy wrapper. I had been so close to Richard Goode in the chapel! I had heard his humming, his feet pressing down on the pedals as he hopped lightly on the bench. The Beethoven sonata he played had seemed a calm musing at first, until the mind took a turn and encountered an object it had desired and lost. A high delicate note was struck, and this was what the heart wanted and kept returning to, the memories hitting as light and quick as rain. Even then, I knew it wouldn't last with Vincent, this is what the music was telling me, yet it made the moment sweeter as we sat close, our shoulders touching, breathing silently together.

After the performance, I walked with a stream of other concertgoers to the BART station and thought about what Sylvia had said to me over the phone. Whenever I saw or read the news about New Orleans now, I thought about her and all that she was going through. "It's like someone shuffled the deck and I've been given a completely different hand," she told me. "I'm constantly sad, but it isn't a lonely sadness. Everyone here has lost something."

I had heard from Clay again. He wrote to tell me he wanted to be friends. He had always liked me for my mind, and that hadn't changed. If I thought he was going to sulk and play the role of rejected suitor, then I was wrong. He invited me to see a movie with him, but I'd seen the trailer already—the hero and heroine contemplating each other scornfully as rain and lust dripped down their faces. I thought this movie was the last one I wanted to see with him and didn't write back.

Vincent also wrote me. He was still swimming laps in the pool every day for his health. I imagined his thin, asymmetrical body and faintly blue feet stretching across the water in melancholy languor. I liked to think of him suspended like this and wondered if his life would turn out light or heavy. But I didn't really want to know. Details only fixed him more clearly in my mind, and I had stopped writing him. Every day, he recedes a little more. In my mind he has become a Sisyphus, fated to move slowly back and forth through the water.

Kate told me I should send out good wishes to people who have hurt or angered me most. "It's a way of letting go of them," she said. "Who knows if your prayers will do them any good? It's a way of finding peace with them in your own mind." Did I wish Vincent and Clay well? I wanted to.

As I rode the subway going home, I noticed another train moving along beside mine. It was like watching a lit theater. I could see the people on the other train so clearly through the windows, and they were doing what people do on trains — sleeping, conversing, reading a newspaper, listening to music, staring into space — but there was an element of unreality to it all as everything unfolded in silence. It was like a pantomime, the actors partially hidden and set apart behind glass, the characters changing as the train slowly advanced beside mine. I saw a woman scratching her neck as she fanned herself, a man putting something away in a bag, a girl gazing out the window with her hand close to her mouth, and I wanted to know their secrets, all the things that are felt and never said. Their train floated parallel to mine, swaying luxuriously from side to side, sometimes falling a little behind or inching slightly ahead, and it seemed like a dance the way the trains moved sideways farther apart and then came close together again. Only when my train slowed down for the next stop could I see how fast the other train was moving as it turned into a silver blur rushing by.

THE MODERN AGE

L ast week my friend Milly invited me to a latke party to
celebrate Hanukkah. All of us sat around her table eating
latkes with applesauce or sour cream, and Milly was telling me
how to make them. "You grate the potato as finely as possible,"
she said. "It's from my mom's belief that the more effort you
put in, the better it will taste. My mom likes to make cooking
a hardship."

Milly's friend Cornelius was fiddling with a knife that he
had picked up from the table. The cunning shape of the blade
bothered me, as if it had been designed for something more
sinister than paring potatoes. He kept turning it over on the
tablecloth, pressing the blade against his thumb. I had heard
that as a child he had undergone heart surgery to correct an
arrhythmia, and now his languid body and swollen hands suggested a slow-pulsing heart. Milly couldn't resist the morbid
gleam of his mind. I had seen them sitting on a bench together
in Rittenhouse Square, Cornelius speaking with his nose to
the sky and his arms crossed over his chest as Milly toyed with

the edge of her coat. My friend had the plain, delicate beauty of a moth—a pale, uncanny face and faded brown hair with a silver streak in front, though she was only twenty-six years old. Her loft apartment was whimsical and spare, a few glass objects lining the high windows.

Cornelius gave the knife a lazy spin. "Let's go around the table and tell each other persecuted ancestor stories." We looked at him in surprise, and he said, "It should be easy. Everyone here is Chinese or Jewish."

Now we looked at one another, as if for the first time, and laughed.

"I'll go first," Cornelius said, and he proceeded to tell us about his great-uncle Frederic who cut off his little toe to escape being drafted.

"I have a story like that," Milly said, "only my grandfather was smarter. He put special drops in his eyes and flunked the eye test to avoid joining the Russian army."

We went around the table, sharing stories we had heard from our families. Jennifer told us about her revolutionary grandmother, a spy for the Guomindang who was captured by the Japanese. Rachel told us about a second cousin of her mother's who was hidden by a Polish farmer underneath the floor of his barn. David told us about his grandfather who walked all the way from Nanjing to Shanghai to escape the Communists.

"In some versions, he takes a train, but the official version is that he walks barefoot across the whole of China." David grinned and straightened his glasses. "When he gets to Shanghai, he has no money left. The Communists are on their way, and my grandfather is afraid he'll be executed because he's a member of the Guomindang. He spends the night under a tree and dreams of a female ghost beneath the ground reaching up to grab him. He wakes up to take a piss, and his stream of urine is so strong it uncovers something shiny from the soil. My grandfather bends down to find a woman's gold ring. The next day he exchanges it for a boat ride to Taiwan, and that's how he escaped the Communists." David smiled at us again, clearing his throat. He was usually a quiet person, and that was the most any of us had heard him say in one evening.

I told them about my mother's uncle, who was beaten and held for ransom by local bandits hiding in the mountains near his village. He was released only when his family delivered a wood coffin filled with coins to his kidnappers.

Cornelius raised his eyebrows. "A coffin?"

I nodded. "His family went bankrupt in order to save him, even though they thought he was a useless person. He was addicted to opium, but when he was released he couldn't afford to smoke it anymore and he became something like a servant to his younger brothers. Every morning he walked my mother to school, and the two of them would search the ground for cigarette stubs. Then he would slit them open and collect the remaining tobacco to make a cigarette for himself."

"What happened to him?" Milly asked.

"No one really knows. He refused to leave when the Communists took over, and my family fled their village and lost track of him."

"Well, all of this makes me think how insignificant my own problems are," Milly said with a little smile. "Here I am complaining about how I don't have a boyfriend and hate my job, but I've never had to worry about anything really. Like I've never had to think about cutting my toe off. It just seems so absurd. Yet all these people had to struggle through so much adversity. And it had to do with when you were born and where you lived. I can't imagine it."

"It's easy to forget how lucky we are," I said.

"Where do you think our sadness comes from?" Cornelius said. "From owning too many things? From indigestion?" He had picked up the knife again and with the tip of it was tracing light circles on the back of his hand. "A person whose struggle, whose suffering, is created internally . . . well, it's just one's feelings, isn't it, one's depression. There isn't anything really to despair about."

"But even so, isn't that person's suffering real?" I asked.

Cornelius gazed at me with pity. There was something cruel about his regard. He believed he could do nothing for me. I experienced a similar hopelessness every morning when I opened up the newspaper. Or when I watched a spider drown in my bathtub.

Milly lit the menorah from left to right, and she, Cornelius, and Rachel sang a blessing in Hebrew with low voices. Their warbling was sweet to hear, and we smiled at each other like children who have entered a magic circle.

I left Milly's party and walked along old narrow streets, feeling a peculiar tenderness as I passed by quaint eighteenth-century homes with their soft-lighted windows. Inside, I imagined lit candles, roses in glass vases, gleaming mirrors, and bowls of potpourri smelling of cinnamon and pears. I imagined those warm rooms and wished more than anything to step inside.

The cold was vivid against my skin. By the time I reached my boyfriend's apartment, I felt I was glowing. I tried to explain to him how interesting it had been, going around the table at Milly's latke party, relating the terrible, miraculous things that had happened to our families. My boyfriend frowned. He is a serious person and wondered if we had told our stories in bad faith, simply to amuse ourselves. When I described to him how Milly made latkes, my boyfriend, who is Jewish, finally cracked: "That's not how my mother makes them!" He has never liked Milly and thinks she is a cold person because she talks to a spot above his head without looking at him. My feelings for her are so different. I have a photograph of her standing under a huge magnolia tree, and she is wearing a blue dress and black Mary Jane shoes, and she looks just like Alice in Wonderland. Even if I show him this picture, my boyfriend will never see Milly as I do.

Then we went to bed. I thought about Milly and Cornelius, and how nothing will ever happen between them. Cornelius is self-absorbed, and Milly, shy and repressed. Both of them are too afraid, but what is it that they are afraid of? As for my boyfriend and me, we had been together for over a year, yet not once had the word *love* been spoken between us. Our hearts seemed too small for such a word to pass between our lips. We had not encountered adversity and seemed fated to walk through life unattached, glancing at one another through distant windows.

INTRUDERS

W hen I was still in my twenties, I lived for a few months in an artist colony in Oregon. Before then, I had never lived by the sea. I don't know what it was I wanted there, but I kept imagining a pale room with glimmering walls. The room would be silent and modest, and if there was any sound it would be muted and far away like the sound of the sea inside a shell. In my vision, the room and its view of the shore were always absent of people.

In March, I arrived at the colony, and the woman in the office handed me a key to my studio. The door turned out to be unlocked, drifting on its hinge. It was early afternoon, yet the room seemed steeped in twilight, the windows shadowed by a view of the stairwell and the parking lot. The room was cluttered with mismatched furniture—a futon covered with gaudy orchids, a narrow bench that served as a coffee table, an oak desk scarred with graffiti, a bright square of blood orange carpet—and the fireplace had long ago been sealed off with white plaster. It was a senseless patchwork of a room, as if composed by a distracted mind. One corner opened up into a dead-end space used for storage, and here I found two coffee machines, a box of handmade Christmas ornaments, the head of a plastic doll, a recent crusty issue of a porn magazine, a flat white clamshell blotted with cigarette ash, and a tin can crammed with stiff, unusable paintbrushes.

I closed the curtains and lay down in bed. Above me, a tile had broken loose like a rotted tooth. It sat on brass pipes, which ran straight across the ceiling and disappeared into the closet.

Someone knocked on the door. It was Steve, the maintenance man, and he asked me how I liked the apartment. "It's kind of dark in there so I made sure to put in plenty of lamps," he said. "There's even one that belonged to my mother-in-law."

I smiled and thanked him. Then I closed the door and returned to bed.

An hour later, I heard another knock.

"Hello," a young man wearing small round spectacles said. "We haven't met. Martin Leung." He extended his hand, and I shook it. He had grayish green eyes and short cropped hair, and there were little gaps between his teeth. He had pulled back his shirt cuffs, which were unbuttoned and flared out loosely, and a number of colored rubber bands circled his wrist. He examined me more closely. "Were you sleeping?"

"No," I said.

"Because there aren't any lights on. What could you be doing in there?"

"I'm thinking."

"Oh, fine," he said. "If that's your story." He closed the screen door on me and began to walk away.

"You don't believe me?" I called out.

He turned, smiling slightly. "I'll let you get back to your nap."

I went back to bed, but this time I couldn't fall asleep. I didn't dare turn on the light because then I would have to look at the ceiling. I must have lain awake for hours like this.

The next morning, before anyone else was up, I walked down Market Street to look at the bay. It was tepid and flat and gray. Overweight seagulls brooded in the sand. I found an eroded brick covered with limpets and carried the cold, heavy thing back to my studio to put on the windowsill. The brick was still sandy, and I rinsed it with water, but the shells, which had been as inert as stones, began to move and rise, cracking loudly like ice. I set the brick on my desk, listening to the cracking until I couldn't bear it, and then I picked up the brick and walked to the bay again and tossed it into the water.

On my way back, I passed through the colony's lounge and heard someone playing Chopin, the notes blurred and tinny and mournful, but the pianist stopped when I entered. "I'm sorry," I said, wishing she would continue, but the woman rose slowly from the bench and regarded me with large, somber eyes. "You're a composer, then?" I asked.

The woman said she was a visual artist. Her name was Andrea.

I lightly pressed a key down with one finger. "Don't you like the way old pianos sound?"

"Well, this one is very out of tune," Andrea said. Her shape and stillness reminded me of those impassive Russian dolls, the ones that open to reveal another smaller doll inside that is exactly alike. This goes on until you reach a doll that is the size of a tiny wooden peg.

I asked Andrea what she was working on at the colony.

"Maybe I'll tell you another time," she said. "When I know you better."

But I didn't think Andrea and I would ever be friends.

. . .

In the mornings, I liked to walk down Market Street, catching glimpses of the bay in between the storefronts, the air pungent, smelling of the sea. I passed by the mailman making his rounds, a woman talking sweetly to her Boston terriers, a man tending roses in his garden, and I didn't have to question anything, my mind as clear and calm as the day.

Then I returned to my studio, made a pot of coffee, and sat down to write. But my window faced the stairwell, and I got distracted watching people climb up and down. Whenever an artist peered into my room, I drew back quickly, pretending not to have noticed. Sometimes I pulled down the shade, but even then I felt I could be *seen*. The walls were thin, as if made out of paper. I could hear voices, entire conversations, a door swinging shut, engines starting, laughter, the crunch of gravel, someone hopping down the stairs, an artist shouting in Italian, the dribble of a basketball . . . One morning I felt I couldn't breathe. I sat at my desk, pressing my hands over my ears, as voices leaked through the little paper box that was my room. I waited for silence. Then I sprang out of my chair and drew back the shade, glancing outside to make sure no one was in sight before opening the door. The sky was gray, and any moment it would begin to rain.

I walked rapidly with my head down, my arms tingling with paralysis. The story I was writing was a puzzle inhabited by mannequins in exquisite clothes. The sentences too were shiny and stiff. The words did not look like words after a while. If I stared at the word *and* long enough, it began to look strange. It didn't look right. I sat down in front of town hall and closed my eyes.

"So how many pages have you written this week?"

I looked up and saw Martin, the person who had knocked on my door when I first arrived at the colony. He stood on the sidewalk, an open book in his hand, which didn't surprise me as he seemed like someone who would have his nose in a book while crossing the street. The first raindrops began to fall, and I got up from the bench. "Are you heading back?" I asked, and we began walking toward the colony.

"So how many? Twenty pages?" Martin said, looking at me. "Ten? Five?" When I continued to be silent, he said, "Two? One?" He stared at me in wonder. "Have you even written a sentence?"

"I write very slowly."

Martin laughed, turning his face to the sky. "I'm so relieved! All this time I thought, she's writing pages and pages! You don't know how worried I was. But why don't you ever come out of your apartment? What are you doing in there all day?"

"Well, I read," I said. "And I think about the story I'm writing."

"So you're working on stories while you're here?"

"Just one."

Martin's eyebrows lifted. "A single story?"

I nodded. There was a light, steady rain now, and we had arrived at our studios, but I didn't want to return to mine. "Let's keep walking."

"All right. But let me drop off my book." In a few minutes, he came out of his studio carrying an umbrella and a mug of coffee.

"So you're miserable here, aren't you?" he said.

"I like living by the sea."

"What's so great about living by the sea?"

"It feels momentous, don't you think?"

"It's supposed to feel momentous, but does it? Are you really moved when you see it?"

"Yes."

"Because I don't feel anything," he said. "I'm supposed to feel something . . . I'm supposed to feel *wonder*." The sidewalk was too narrow for both of us, and he began walking down the middle of the street as he talked, looking at me over the parked cars. Midsentence, and a van would completely obscure him from view. "Because the only sincere response I can have is if I don't expect it. There's a road here in town that I like because of the way it rises. You go up and up this hill, and when you're least expecting it, all of a sudden there it is—the sea—and I feel the seaness of the sea. For a moment. As soon as I become aware of it, the feeling passes."

"The seaness of the sea."

"I said that, didn't I? It's brilliant, isn't it? The seaness of the sea!" He finished drinking his coffee and put the mug in his coat pocket.

My hair and shoes were drenched now, and my scarf felt twice as long around my neck, yet I didn't mind. I liked how the rain made everything vivid, as if my eyes were clearer and the world more sharply focused. The sidewalk glistened, and the cars on the street looked newly polished. We walked for a moment in silence, staring at the bay.

"Well, this is all slightly unreal," Martin said, "isn't it?"

The next morning, I heard a soft rapping at my door. It was Andrea, grave and inscrutable, her thick arms curved around her stomach. She wore oversize glasses, and her dark brown hair spread out from her face in the shape of a mushroom. She asked me if I could take her to the grocery store.

In the car, I asked if she enjoyed living at the colony.

"Yes," she replied, looking out the window.

"It's pretty here, isn't it?"

"I guess you could say that."

At Safeway, Andrea pushed her cart slowly down the long gleaming aisles. Her face remained expressionless as she delicately picked items off the shelf. She was a short, heavy woman who handled things gently, as if they were alive. At the checkout stand, she carefully pried loose a copy of *Star* magazine from its bin.

When we were back at the colony, I invited myself into her apartment. "Can I see it? I'm curious what the other places look like."

"Susan," she said, and her voice for the first time had a wryness to it. "You are a curious person."

I laughed. "Is there anything wrong with that?" I helped carry her groceries to her door.

"Well, you know, curiosity killed the cat." But she let me inside.

Her apartment was pleasant and bright and clean. She didn't have many things, but everything was neatly arranged. There was a quilt on the bed, her books stood straight on the shelf, and there were no dirty dishes in the sink. A vase of yellow daffodils sat on her kitchen table.

"You keep it so neat."

"I like to know where everything is." She paused for a moment. "Just in case," she added.

"In case of what?"

"Intruders." She turned the radio to a classical station. It was a piano piece, intricate and relentless. The person played with such cold, passionate precision that I felt uneasy. The music threatened to slip away from the pianist's fingers into chaos, yet never did. There was a kind of ruthlessness in such playing. We listened for a few minutes, and then Andrea turned off the radio.

"I hope one day you'll play something for me," I told her.

"I can't play in front of people," she said, bending over to untie her shoelaces. "It makes me nervous, and I begin to make mistakes." She slipped off her shoes and put them in the closet.

"We have the same taste," I said. "I have the same shoes as you do."

"Yes," Andrea said. "I already noticed that. Thank you for taking me shopping." She led me to the door, and as I turned to say good-bye she was already closing it behind me. Then I heard the click of the bolt turning.

During my second week at the colony, a writer invited all the artists to his studio one evening to celebrate his birthday. I arrived late, just as he blew out the candles. I poured myself a glass of wine and sat down alone on the couch. An artist gazed at me sympathetically from across the table. I smiled at her and cut myself a piece of cake even though I didn't want to eat it.

The artist, whose name was Karine, asked me how my work was going, and I nodded my head, eating the cake messily with my fingers. Then she asked, "Do you have a boyfriend or a husband?"

"Neither," I replied.

Karine tilted her head, studying me closely. "How funny that you should be so concerned!" she said. I was startled to see a black spot on the blue of her iris, as if she had held a pen to her eye and stained it with ink.

"Look over there at Elise! Isn't that funny?" She pointed to a poet who stood to the side wearing a plastic brace around her stomach. I thought she was wearing it to be unconventional until Karine told me that Elise had cracked her back a week before while Rollerblading. "Every time I see her wearing that thing, I want to laugh," she said. "Is this your first time at the colony?"

"Yes."

"That's what I thought. You'll find it interesting here. Of course, that's what makes it painful too, but why else do people keep coming back year after year? We tend to poison our own well here, but you shouldn't take it personally."

When I got up from the couch, I knocked over an empty beer bottle that someone had placed on the floor. Martin paused in the middle of his conversation to look at me. "Susan," he said, as if he were trying to steady me, and then he turned away to talk to another writer.

I went over to the table and refilled my glass of wine. "Are you okay?" the host asked me. "You look as if you're about to cry."

"I'm fine," I said, but the question defeated me. I picked up my coat and headed for the door. I found Andrea sitting by herself on the steps outside.

"Are you leaving?" she asked. "I'll go back with you."

We walked along Irving Street in silence. A lone car passed, and everything paled under the headlights. In the momentary glare, we seemed to be the stark negatives of ourselves. It was a relief to be outside, away from the heat of other bodies and the sound of other voices. The car passed, and in the darkness I could expand again. The stars were cold pinpoints of light separated by darkness, and I remembered as a child wanting to pluck them from the sky like jewels. Now as I gazed at the sky, I knew I was seeing the light of dead stars.

Andrea too was silent, and I looked at her face with its wide, blunted cheekbones. She had an immunity, a deep-rooted stubbornness never to smile in order to please others. Her invulnerability resided in her lack of feeling. When I thought about what was inside of her, I could never think literally—organs and blood—but thought of cold, vast space, like the night sky above our heads. Was that what Andrea was like? Or was it like falling through an emptiness?

"So what do you do with yourself all day?" Martin asked me. He was carefully untwisting the ends of foil around the tilapia. "Not done yet," he said, poking at the fish with a knife and then putting it back in the oven.

I sat at his desk and pressed a few keys on his Underwood. "What do you mean?"

"Well, I mean that you stay in that box of an apartment of yours and rarely crawl out."

"I crawled out tonight to come here, didn't I?"

"Yeah, whatever," Martin said, abruptly getting out of his chair. He began swearing at his smoking oven, and I felt my vision blur and the room get smaller. He wasn't nice at all. A tyrant. Martin peered into his oven and slammed the door shut.

"So you still haven't answered my question," he said. "How much of your time do you spend thinking and how much of your time do you spend doing?"

I jabbed at a key with one finger. "I'm sick of thinking. I want my mind to be empty."

"Why would you want that?" he asked. "That happens when you're dead. When you're dead, you have all the time in the world for your mind to be empty."

"But don't you like to sleep?"

"No. What a waste of time." He told me that when he slept, he left the radio on, tuned to the BBC. He didn't want his mind to rest. As he slept, he would hear about all the things going on in the world. His mind would be absorbing words and places. Like Ulaanbaatar, which was the capital of Mongolia.

This struck me as funny and admirable and also a little sad.

We ate the tilapia, which was excellent, and then Martin poured each of us a cup of coffee. "Do you think," he said, placing the sugar bowl in front of me, "that we are just lazy or overly scrupulous as writers?"

"Both."

"That's the problem with you. I'm always trying to make distinctions, and you're always collapsing things together." He picked up the letter opener from his desk and used it to stir his coffee. "I'm sick to death of earnest writing," he said, rapping the metal blade against his cup. "Do you hear that? Everyone hits the same note. It's always about sadness. How sad I am. But try saying 'abyss' three times with a straight face. These morbid writers who can only write about their mother dying! What I want to know is why is everyone so depressed? Hardly anyone ever writes about joy anymore. You know why? Because it's harder to write about joy. It's easier to hit the note of sadness than anything else."

We talked for several hours, and when I finally glanced at my watch it was two a.m. Did he want me to go? He pointed to the narcissus that an artist had given him, a cluster of tiny white flowers framed by long slender leaves, the roots supported by smooth gray and brown stones. It reminded me of the artist's work, which also had that kind of simplicity and neatness. He turned off the light in the kitchen. "See how the flower appears?" he said. "At first, you can't see anything. But then you see it emerge."

"What do you mean?"

He turned the light back on. "Look at the flower," he said. Then he turned off the light. At first I saw nothing, only darkness, and then the narcissus took form. It seemed to be growing white. "Did you see it?" he asked.

"Yes."

Martin flicked on the light.

"Do it again," I said.

Martin turned off the light, and in the darkness we watched the narcissus take on its luminous shape. It floated before us, the ghost of a flower. "Whose is it?" he said. "Who gets to use this?"

"It's yours," I told him. "You observed it."

"How about whichever one of us writes it first?"

"All right." I looked at him. "It's because of our eyes."

"Our pupils are adjusting." He turned on the light. "Isn't it interesting to think that our pupils aren't really black?" he said eagerly, taking a step toward me. "It's just emptiness. There isn't anything there, just a hole."

I couldn't help but stare into his pupils. "I hadn't thought of it like that before," I murmured. I didn't want to go, but it seemed I couldn't stay. He stood near me, looking both formidable and innocent in his white T-shirt, and I wished him good night.

In my studio, I climbed into bed and stared at the crumpled tissue on my night table before turning off the light.

It was quiet in town. The tourists had not yet arrived, and many of the stores were still closed from the winter. I had spent the entire day in the library, surrounded by rows of dark and bright spines, and when I stepped outside, the afternoon had disappeared and the sky was the color of a bruise. The sea glimmered darkly. I could see bare patches of shore under a few cold lights, the relentless electric glare of them.

In my story, the mannequins had changed into more sensual clothes. I had worked over my sentences for so long that they had acquired a fateful sound. Now everything was sealed under a layer of varnish. If I changed anything, the rest would begin to crack.

I found Andrea sitting on the futon in my studio. "The door was unlocked," she said. "The wind blew it open."

I had left my diary open on my desk, and I wondered if Andrea had glanced at the pages. If so, she would know that my thoughts were trivial and cruel.

"Do you want some tea?" I asked.

"No, I just want to sit here." Her hands rested in her lap, and her eyes were glassy and strange. It seemed as though she hadn't moved for hours.

"Andrea, is everything okay?"

"Well, I think someone was in my apartment." She spoke in a neutral voice and sounded unsurprised that such a thing should happen to her. "My stuff was moved around. It was very subtle, but I notice small details like that."

I asked if I should call the police.

"What's the point? There isn't anything missing."

"But why would anyone break in?"

"Well, you know, maybe they were looking for something. Like the number of my checking account."

"You should ask Steve to change your lock."

Andrea shrugged. "I guess." We fell silent, listening to the wind as it shook the windows. Finally, Andrea rose from the couch. "I'm going to bed now."

"Do you want to walk across the breakwater tomorrow?" I asked.

She stood silently in the room, studying the only painting on the wall, a still life of fruit and flowers. I thought she hadn't heard me, but then she turned and looked at me sadly. "All right," she said with a little smile.

"That painting was already here when I came," I said. "Do you think it's any good?" In truth, I felt a little sick whenever I looked at it. It was supposed to be a still life, but the things in the painting threatened to move if I stared hard enough. The apples, pears, and grapes were anemic in their thin wash of color, floating above the bowl without touching it. Beside the pale levitating fruit stood a vase of orange and purple zinnias, their faces heavy and luxuriant yet detached from their stems. At any moment, a brilliant orange head would fall into the bowl—and then what would happen?

I told Andrea that I didn't really like the painting.

"It's something to look at," Andrea replied.

The next morning, Andrea and I walked to the breakwater at the south end of town. Huge irregular stone slabs formed a seawall that ran straight across the bay and ended at the tip of the cape. Though the topmost stones appeared to be flat, once Andrea and I were actually on the breakwater they dipped and slanted like badly crooked teeth. I began jumping from one rock to another, but when I turned around, Andrea was far behind, halted on a rock and staring down at her feet.

"Andrea?"

"Yes," she said, taking one cautious step. She paused and examined the rocks carefully.

"Do you want to go back?"

She shook her head. "I just want to make sure of the rocks."

I walked back and held out my hand. She took it, and we proceeded across the breakwater like this, stopping and starting, in a slow and painful crawl. We passed by stones where seagulls had feasted, littered with iridescent shards of mussels and the half-eaten, translucent bodies of crabs. Toward the end of the breakwater, we saw more abandoned, shipwrecked things—fragments of painted wood, a plastic detergent bottle, a Styrofoam cooler. I was relieved when we finally stepped off the breakwater and began climbing the dunes, past long stems of beach grass that had traced circles in the sand. We went over the rise, and there all at once was the vast glinting blueness of ocean, a deeper blue more piercing than the bay. Andrea and I sat down on the beach with our faces toward the sun, and I felt pleasantly exhausted, listening to the sound of the waves.

"Do you see microscopic things in the sky?" Andrea asked me.

I looked at her and laughed. "What did you just say?"

"When you look at the sky, do you see things like tiny black threads?" Andrea paused, squinting. "I guess they're distortions of your eye. It's like you have to look a certain way at the surface of your eyes."

I stared at the sky, so bright and pure, its blueness verging with the sea. I saw nothing at first. Then I stared harder and narrowed my eyes. Black filaments, like strands of hair, rose and fell into the ocean. I blinked, and the black threads swooped like a flock of birds.

"There are also these points of light," Andrea said.

I looked until the sky began to sparkle slowly. Little crosses or stars. I laughed and told Andrea I was seeing visions. I felt happy in the way you do when another world has been opened to you.

"This is how I occupy myself when I'm feeling bored," Andrea said.

I stretched out and closed my eyes, sinking further into the warm oblivion of sun and sand. My eyelids could not shut out the radiance, and I felt I was dreaming, my body turning into light and air. When I opened my eyes, I saw the same view of beach and sky, more vivid and distinct than anything I could have imagined or remembered.

Andrea's voice was as low and insistent as the surf receding from the shore. "Do you sometimes have moments," Andrea said, "in which you're walking down a street and everything is normal, but then for no reason at all everything takes a turn and things become unreal? It's like you're more distant from the world. Detached. And everything is new, more present. It's like the surfaces of things have been peeled away, and you're seeing something, trying to understand it, for the first time." She picked up a pebble and placed it in the palm of her hand. "I don't know why I'm saying this," she said. She searched in the sand for more pebbles, and then showed them to me. "What do you think?"

There were three pebbles in her hand, a translucent yellow, a rose, and a milky gray. "Very pretty," I said.

"I think I'll take these home."

"Are you going to look for seashells?"

"I'm not so interested in those."

It was midafternoon by the time we crossed over the breakwater again and returned to town. When we were two blocks away from the colony, I spotted Martin ahead of us, turning down Laurel Street. I quickened my pace, hoping to catch up with him, but Andrea would not be hurried, and I had to slow down. We drew closer, and I realized I had been mistaken. It was not Martin at all but someone taller and thinner, with a frayed satchel and a patch of fabric on the seat of his pants. The man walked slowly ahead of us, like a convalescent, a gentleness about him that made me want to step lightly behind. An older woman approached, and he stopped to talk to her, showing her his book.

"Martin!" I said, and he turned around to look at us. Even now, I don't know why I had ever doubted it was him. Yet he had seemed different walking up the hill alone. The woman said good-bye, smiling at me as she passed.

"You know," Martin said, his eyes widening slightly as he tapped me on the arm with his book. "I wanted to tell you something. Something to do with a discovery of mine about the seaness of the sea."

"What is it?"

"Oh, it's too long to go into now."

"What are you reading?"

He showed me the cover of his book.

"But you've already read *The Waves*," I said.

"Well, you know," he said, shrugging slightly. "It's the novel of *despair*."

I laughed, and we talked about Virginia Woolf as Andrea walked silently beside us. When we arrived at the colony, Andrea moved away without saying good-bye, and I felt sorry for having forgotten her. "Andrea," I said, "are you going already?"

She put the can of Coke she had been drinking into the trash. "Well, I can go," she said in her quiet, acerbic way, and she climbed the stairs slowly and retreated to her studio.

• • •

In April, the visual artists at the colony had a group show at the local art museum. Everyone crowded into the Driftwood Tavern for food and drinks an hour before the opening. Tea candles spread out before us like stars, and I sat between Martin and Andrea, the three of us looking down the long table at the other artists immersed in conversation. All these lit, transmuted faces. A napkin caught on fire in front of me, and I stared at it until a filmmaker extinguished it in his hands. Everyone clapped. When we asked if he had burned himself, he said that his skin was resistant to flames.

Martin was intently cutting his chicken when he asked Karine, who sat across from him, "If you could push the art button or the happiness button, which would you choose?"

"The art button, of course," she replied coolly. "Who here believes in happiness?"

Then I asked, "Who do you think is happiest here among us?"

Martin began to rank the people at the table, from the most depressed to the most happy. He put me toward the bottom of the list near the people who we knew were manic-depressives, and he put himself toward the top. When he mentioned Andrea's name, I glanced at her, wondering if she was listening, but she only continued eating her steak and sipping her wine with the calm inevitability that marked everything she said or did. "Andrea is healthy and immune!" Martin declared. "She goes to the top of the list!"

"How do you know that, Martin?" Andrea said quietly, looking at him. "You don't know me. Or anyone else at this table. How can you know something like that?"

Martin's eyes softened, and the rest of us fell silent. We could hear the uneven patter of rain outside, and from the window we saw silver glints falling. A few, including Martin, pushed back their chairs and went out to smoke, and I whispered to Andrea that Martin was only teasing.

"Susan, I would be grateful if you didn't tell Martin my business," she replied.

As we walked to the museum, Andrea stayed close beside me, carrying her funereal umbrella. "What is it you don't like about Martin?" I asked her.

"He talks too much."

"What's wrong with that?"

Andrea looked at me. "Martin says a thing, but it doesn't mean he believes it."

"You don't trust him."

"Charming people are always the worst." We had arrived at the museum, but Andrea informed me that she was going home.

"But we just got here. Shouldn't you be at your own opening?"

"It's a group show. I'm not showing anything anyway." When I stared at her, she gave a slight shrug. "People like your work, people don't like your work. Then they stand around telling you why." She turned away, and I watched as she tread carefully down the street, every now and then glancing down at her feet as though she expected the ground to split open and something to leap out at her.

In the museum, I stared at a defunct radiator whose bland surface Karine had decorated with neat rows of lip imprints. The lips were all the same — Karine's? — but the color of lipsticks varied like the shades of flowers. "Where did you get the radiator?" I asked when she passed by.

Karine's eyes widened. "I love your reaction!" she said. "That is precisely the reaction I wanted to get. The radiator is part of this *very* room. It is a fully functioning radiator. You never noticed it before, did you? I'm so glad. I wanted you to pay attention to the physical space we're in, to make you really *see* the things you normally are blind to."

I nodded, at a loss as to what to say next, and Karine took my hand. "You're so funny, you know that? Always asking questions and smiling and saying 'pardon me' and 'thank you.'" She dropped my hand abruptly and darted away into the crowd.

I saw Martin enter the room, momentarily pause to look around him as he toyed with the loose button on his coat. He was the person whose presence I desired most, yet I could not bring myself to go up to him. I walked around the museum, pretending to look at the art, until he approached me. "So how many times have you sighed and looked up at the sky today?" he asked, lifting the end of my scarf and placing it on top of his nose.

"What did you just say?" I was worried that my scarf smelled of rain or mildew.

"My God, you only hear half the things I say to you, isn't that right?" He laughed. "I'm too fast for you! I'm running circles around you!" And right there in the museum, he began to run in place. "So where has your plucky companion gone off to?" he asked, coming to a sudden stop.

"Andrea?"

"Your chatty friend and I have butted heads before. Do you know she tried to slam the door on my finger when I visited her studio?"

"She values her privacy."

It was too crowded to talk in the museum, and we left the show early, heading back toward the colony. "Andrea is like a stone," Martin said. "I don't know what's worse. Is it better to be numb to the world or overly sensitive to it?"

I stopped. "It's better to feel too much, of course." Martin looked back at me in surprise, and I laughed and took his arm. We walked back to my studio like this, my arm linked through his.

"I always think there's something occult going on whenever I pass by your place," he said as he entered, looking around him. He sat down at my desk and opened my drawers, examining their contents before slamming them shut again. He got up to inspect the books on my mantel, and when I returned with cups of tea, he was slipping a paperback into his coat pocket. "I'm stealing your Maupassant," he informed me.

"All right," I said, handing him his cup. I hadn't any clean spoons, and he stirred his tea with a pen lying on the coffee table. "That isn't sterile," I said gravely.

"Ha! I am not a sterile person!" he declared, and he leaned over to kiss me. It was lovely and strange to finally touch him. His skin was soft and warm, smelling of cloves and soap and cigarettes, and I could do nothing to make the sensation less immediate, my mind slower than my body, as if emerging from a thick fog. Martin pulled me toward him, then just as suddenly released me, climbed over the futon, and yanked the lamp cord out of its socket.

The next morning I looked out my window and saw Martin fixing his car in the parking lot. He had a pitiless look about him, a forthright, unsmiling intensity, and seemed closed off in his own world. It was hard to believe anything had happened between us. I watched as he scraped beneath the hood of his car with methodical ferocity.

We passed by each other in the mailroom, and Martin

greeted me with an ironic smile, which I reflected faithfully back. "Hello, Susan."

"Hello, Martin."

We retreated to our separate studios.

I couldn't work. My whole being was set at a higher pitch, but what did this matter to Martin or anyone else? People knocked on your door, entered your space, then ruined your peace. I left my studio and walked down Market Street to clear my head. The sky was vertiginously blue, and the road and trees seemed to glow and vibrate. The locals and tourists were out riding their bicycles, sipping their coffee, reading the daily newspaper, and I felt that I was seeing everything from the eyes of a child or a drug addict. The world's sharp beauty wouldn't leave me alone. It was difficult just to cross the street.

I returned to my studio and found a piece of paper wedged into my screen door. It was a scribbled note from Martin, asking if I cared to go fishing.

Martin picked me up that afternoon, and we drove to a beach outside of town. He had brought along an extra fishing rod, which I tried to use, but it took me only a few minutes to tangle my line. Martin cast his rod sternly as if it were a whip, and in the rigid way he held himself I sensed how much he demanded from the world. Nothing would ever be easy for him. Now and then he glanced at me shyly, and I knew he felt self-conscious with me there watching.

I set down my pole and began walking. Tiny starfish had washed up along the shore, their arms contorted at various angles. They were not brittle or light but a surprising weight in my palm, all the water and life still in them. I put them down and kept walking. Sandpipers and gulls moved out of my path.

When I turned around, Martin was a tiny sand-colored figure against the horizon.

The tide was coming in by the time I returned. Tiny fish were leaping out of the water and pockmarking the surface like rain. Martin had caught a thin herring, its back tinged with pink and green. It lay on the sand, and when a wave came in, almost taking the fish away, I scooped it up, its scales smearing onto my hand like silver flecks of paint.

The sky darkened, and it felt uneasy between us as we drove back to the colony. "Sometimes, when I see you outside, you're entirely different," I said. "You're terse and brusque and aggressive."

"Hey, I have things to do."

"But other times, you are completely sweet and even mild. It's like there are two Martins. I never know which one to expect."

"Well, you need the one in order to appreciate the other. Which do you like better?"

"I like both," I said hopelessly.

He smiled a little at this, staring ahead at the road. "Do you think we get along?" he mused. He glanced over at me. "Perhaps we don't truly get along."

"We do," I said, but his question hurt.

There was an awkward pause, and then Martin said he had not smoked a cigarette for a week and that he was going crazy. When I suggested candy or nicotine patches, he blew up at me. "Can't I have this experience on my own?" he demanded. He thought he should go cold turkey. He wanted to savor how difficult it was to quit in order to have the full experience of not smoking.

"You are the most difficult person I know," I said. "You make everything complex."

"But I want the opposite of complexity," he said. "I am try-ing to have an experience that is not mediated by anything else." He parked the car, and we sat in gloomy silence. "It's like this," he said, taking his key out of the ignition and pressing it against the windshield. "I want to touch this glass, but I am touching this key that is touching this glass. So I am not touch-ing this glass at all."

"Why do you have to analyze everything? Everything is a struggle for you," I said bitterly. In truth, I was sick of artists. I was tired of complexity and contradiction, of sensitive people saying remarkable, nuanced things.

Martin opened his door to signal that our conversation was at an end. I trembled as I stepped out of his car. "Well, *hasta luego,* Susan," Martin said rather breezily.

"Thank you for taking me fishing," I said stiffly.

"Yes," he paused. "Good night, Susan."

There is a pleasure in having secrets, an inner life that no one knows anything about. I like the impassive face I present to the world even though I may feel a burning inside. To tell some-one about my pain is to give it up. Or worse, I would have to see it grow small in the eyes of others. But not to tell anyone means that none of it has a life outside my head.

I gave an informal reading with two other writers in the colony lounge one afternoon at the end of April. Afterward Karine tapped me on the shoulder. "You are a sly one, aren't you?" she said.

"What do you mean?" I asked, and I thought she knew about me and Martin.

"You're not as innocent as you look, my dear. You can pre-tend no longer with me. I always thought you were so nice and shy, but all the while there were these merciless thoughts going on inside your head. I'm afraid of you now."

I looked into Karine's eyes. "Everyone always says I'm nice, but they never mean it as a compliment. I'm not *nice*. I don't think I am."

"You don't *think* you are," she said, smiling.

Martin was nowhere in sight. I assumed he had left early because he didn't like my work and didn't want to compromise himself by saying untruthful things about it. I felt restless and decided to visit Andrea in her studio. She was knitting a scarf and watching television, a glass of water on the table in front of her. The vase that I had seen filled with daffodils was now empty of flowers. I sat down beside her, blinking at the television screen, where characters with the same cloying beauty loved each other under the warm California light. During a commercial, I asked Andrea how she could stand watching this stuff.

"I don't take it too seriously," she replied.

"But why not watch something good?"

"I get tired of meaningfulness."

We went out for coffee and afterward sat on the beach, listening to the beating of the ocean. There was a wild, desolate smell of brine and broken shells, and strewn along the shore were moon jellies and huge tuberous roots that looked like serpents disgorged from the sea. Not far from us a ravaged seagull stuck out from the sand.

I forgot myself, then remembered myself.

Andrea was shaping mounds of sand with slow, careful hands. "Do you think there's something funny about this town?"

The wind was sharp and cold, and I sat up, wrapping my arms tight around me. "What do you mean?"

"I noticed a man sitting at the table next to us at the café. He was looking at me, and I felt peculiar, like maybe I had seen him before. And then I remembered I *had* seen him before. A week before, he was standing in line behind me at the bank." Andrea was silent for a moment. "Both times he said something about me."

"What did he say?"

"In the bank he said, 'She looks all right, but you never know.' And in the café, he said, 'She thinks highly of herself, doesn't she?' "

"Why would he be talking about you?"

Andrea shrugged. "Sometimes when I'm walking down Market Street, I feel there's a subtle pattern to the people coming toward me and the people following behind. It seems to be random, these people walking on the street, but it's not. It's like everyone is pretending to be jogging or walking a dog or looking at a store window, everyone is pretending to be going on with their own lives. But all the while they're interested, they're watching me and picking me apart. I always pretend I don't notice anything, but everyone is just waiting for you to give yourself away. People say terrible things about you." Andrea's eyes had a glassy sheen, though her face remained stony and impenetrable.

"But how do you know they're talking about you?" I asked.

Andrea frowned slightly. "Well, I hear them." She looked down at her hands. "I shouldn't have said all this," she said quietly.

"No, I'm glad you did."

"You probably think I should be in the loony bin."

"No, I don't think that." But I felt a chill inside me, a sick, empty feeling as if all at once I was falling.

"I don't know what it is about you, Susan. But I always spill my guts out to you."

"I don't know either," I said, and we laughed.

We stayed on the beach for another hour, lying on the sand like paralytics. The incessant murmur of the ocean grew inside my head until it resembled a clamor of voices. The beach was gleaming, burning. The world seemed unbearable in its light. It was hard to believe that any two people shared a reality between them. I felt myself entering my own reality as if it were a tunnel or a dream. I know now you lose yourself by going deeper. It is a hole you slip down. You think you are getting closer to truth when actually your mind reveals nothing.

Andrea left the colony soon after. She didn't tell anyone she was taking off but simply packed her things and called a cab in the middle of the night while the rest of us were asleep. I discovered a note from her written inside my diary, her print as neat and careful as a schoolgirl's. *It is no longer safe for me to stay here. You may think it's all in my head what I told you. For the longest time I thought so too. But one day something caught my attention. An odd detail I picked up. I examined it more closely and now I can't forget. If you peel back just a little corner of things, you will see. I wanted to tell you.*

She didn't sign the note, and I tore the page out of my diary because it began to look strange the more I stared at it. I didn't want Andrea's thoughts to be mistaken for my own. That night I dreamed of her. She was lying next to me in bed, and we shared a flimsy, moth-eaten blanket. When I woke up, it was past midnight. I folded Andrea's note into my pocket and left the studio, walking across the yard toward Martin's cottage.

We hadn't truly spoken to each other since the night in the parking lot, and I hesitated before knocking on his door.

"Come in!" Martin yelled.

I was surprised to find him lying on the couch, his eyeglasses pushed back over his head, a red imprint on his cheek.

"You were sleeping!" I said to him, and it made me glad to think that even he had to let his mind rest, to be vulnerable as he slipped into unconsciousness. The apartment exuded a drowsy warmth. The lights were still on, and the windows had turned cloudy from the cold outside. Martin blinked as he tried to sit up from the couch.

"Don't get up," I said, kneeling down beside him. "Stay there."

He gave a little sigh and closed his eyes. He wrapped the blanket more closely around him. "When I sleep," he said, "I want to enshroud myself. Before you go to sleep, everything— the room, the furniture—begins to swirl around, to spin . . ."

"Like Proust," I said.

"Like Proust." He opened one eye. "I heard your partner in crime disappeared. Where did she run off to?"

I thought about Andrea's note in my pocket, but I didn't show it to him. "I don't know."

"You and Andrea. You both are immune."

"No," I said. "Neither of us is immune."

"Immune," he repeated.

"That's not true." I placed my palm against his forehead, and he closed his eyes.

"You are a cold woman," he said.

"I'm not."

"Cold," he repeated, but his lips smiled faintly, as if he were dreaming.

I moved out of the colony at the end of May. I never did finish my story and left the drafts behind in a box in the dead-end storage space of my studio.

Sometimes I received postcards from Martin hastily clacked out on his Underwood. The letters were always animated, full of misspellings and unfinished sentences. He lived in the present, and other faces delighted him. I imagined his conversations unfolding slowly through the night, taking shape by dawn. He said his greatest sympathies lay with Neville in *The Waves,* but I always thought of him as Bernard, rushing off to catch the next train without a ticket.

I saw Andrea again two years later, after I had moved to New York. It was on a foggy December morning as I was coming out of my studio in Brooklyn. The city seemed insubstantial, barely formed in the pale morning light. She was bent over on the sidewalk tying her shoe, her face obscured by her thick hair. "Andrea," I said, and she straightened up and looked at me with a solemn smile. The glasses she wore took up half her face. "Andrea," I repeated, but she turned away and began walking down the street. I followed her a few steps and touched her arm. "Won't you say anything?" I asked her. "Why don't you speak to me?" But she kept walking with her head down, though the curious smile remained on her lips, and finally I let her go, watching her disappear into the traffic on the street.

GARDEN CITY

No one wanted to rent the Chens' apartment. It sat vacant for three months, collecting dust and heat. Footsteps now and then echoed along the wood floors. Voices came and went. Sometimes the drone of a fly butting itself against glass. Until silence fell, and the fly— its legs as thin as eyelashes—dried on the kitchen windowsill.

In August, when Mr. Chen opened the door, he felt the apartment's hot breath as he entered, the Christian lady following behind. The windows had become as cruel as a magnifying glass. Mr. Chen's head swam, as if it were severed from his body and floating in the ocean. He blinked, trying to see the woman more clearly.

"A good apartment, this one," he heard himself saying. "Everything paid for. Garbage. Electricity."

His eyes were watering. For a moment, he could not remember what he was going to say. He walked over to the windows and began pulling down the blinds. Light glinted off cars and trees from the parking lot.

"Garden also," Mr. Chen murmured.

His wife called the apartment their worst investment. "Other than you and I getting married, this apartment has been the biggest mistake of our lives," she said.

No one wanted to live there. The rent was too high, even though the Chens kept lowering their price, stopping at eight hundred to break even. People called, but lost interest when they heard it wasn't near the subway station. The ones who actually saw the apartment examined the scratched floors, smiled politely at the 1970s plastic cabinets, inquired whether there was a dishwasher. There wasn't. Washing machine? Dryer? Mr. Chen shook his head. The laundromat was next door. After that, there was only the bedroom left to see. This was the moment Mr. Chen dreaded the most. He always felt an urge to apologize for how small it was. The previous owner had called it "quaint" when he showed it to the Chens eight years ago. If the people were kind, they went through the motions of opening the closet door and peering inside. A short while later, they thanked Mr. Chen, saying they would think about it. The door closed, and Mr. Chen was left standing alone in the apartment. He was a stout man, but at such moments his body seemed to cave in, as if his bones were softening. The apartment was quiet and hollowed out. A part of him wanted to rest on the dull wood floor, the same color as earth. He didn't want to go home to his wife and tell her of another failure.

They had bought the apartment because Mr. Chen thought it would be safe to invest in real estate. It wasn't like the stock market, where you bought what you couldn't touch, your money rising and falling with intangible economic winds. Mr. Chen had a literal mind. He promised his wife that they would earn four or even five hundred dollars a month once they paid off the mortgage. He hadn't realized that the apartment management would raise their maintenance fee every year, that the value of the property would fall, and that no one would be interested in renting. It was a bad sign that most of the people living there were the apartment owners themselves.

When Mr. Chen thought about it carefully, he was convinced that he had been fooled into buying the apartment. He blamed the garden, a conservatory adjoining the lobby, which was always pungent with the smell of overripe flowers. Eight years earlier, he and Mrs. Chen had been beguiled by the magenta-speckled lilies as they sat together on one of the wooden benches. Mr. Chen had gotten out of his seat once or twice, pacing the garden in an excited manner. "Who wouldn't want to live here?" he said in Chinese to his wife.

Mrs. Chen knew that her husband was naïve, that he had a habit of promising things he couldn't deliver. When he began exaggerating, her lips would wrinkle in disgust. "Don't be ridiculous," she would say, waving her hand impatiently in front of her face. Sitting in the garden, however, Mrs. Chen was distracted by the huge lavender peonies that looked as clear and delicate as watercolors. She couldn't help but be lulled by the fragrances wafting beneath her tingling nose as she listened to her husband's boastful talk, all his plans for them and their son. She could not deny that the garden was a beautiful thing. In the end, she agreed that they should invest their savings in the apartment.

Eight years had gone by, and their son was now dead. Whenever Mrs. Chen saw the garden, she felt a bitterness rise up to her mouth. The smell of lilies reminded her of funerals now. Their rich, exhausting perfume made her want to claw at her throat. The transplanted flowers were crowded too close together, and their thin, transparent petals gave off a ghostly luster. This was not a living garden, Mrs. Chen decided. Not a place where things came back.

When he first met the Christian lady, Mr. Chen was startled by the coldness of her fingers. He wondered if she had poor circulation. She slipped her bony hand out from his, glancing quickly around the lobby. She wore a dark blue suit in spite of the heat and a thin white blouse with faux-pearl buttons. Though she was respectably dressed, the suit was too large for her and made her seem almost pitiful, as if she were wearing another person's clothes.

When Mr. Chen first called the woman to set up an appointment, he got her answering machine. A listless recorded voice spoke to him. *And God shall wipe away all tears from their eyes; and there shall be no more death, neither sorrow, nor crying, neither shall there be any more pain.* There was a pause and then a beep. Mr. Chen hung up the phone, for some reason too embarrassed to leave a message. He called back later that night after he and Mrs. Chen had closed the grocery store.

A soft voice answered the phone.

"Yes. Hello," he said abruptly. "I am calling you back. You say you interested in the apartment? Garden City Apartments, 26 Harrison."

Mrs. Chen listened on the extension as her husband spoke. It was a constant regret of hers that she had not married a more cultured man. Mr. Chen's brusqueness always became more apparent when he spoke English. It was even worse when he was on the phone, for then he shouted his responses as if he were deaf. What must these Americans think? she wondered. The woman said she was interested. Her name was Marnie Wilson, and she agreed to meet Mr. Chen at noon the next day. Mrs. Chen heard a click at the other end as the American lady hung up, and then she, too, put down the receiver.

"Did you hear?" Mr. Chen said to his wife.

"Yes," Mrs. Chen said, "but will she rent it? Bargain with her if you have to, but don't show her you're desperate. That will only scare her away."

Mr. Chen remembered his wife's words now as he stood in front of the shaded windows of the apartment, nodding and smiling at the Christian lady. He noticed that she stepped gingerly around the empty rooms, as if she were afraid of setting off echoes with her heels. Mr. Chen judged that she was twenty-six, maybe twenty-seven years old. Her formality and meekness made her seem old-fashioned. Maybe she came from another country, though to Mr. Chen's ear she spoke perfect English.

As they rode down in the elevator to see the garden, Mr. Chen learned that the Christian lady worked as a receptionist at World Wide Travel. Had Mr. Chen heard of it? The office was only three or four blocks away. Mr. Chen said he had not. He didn't know of any office buildings close by. The woman wrapped her hand tighter around her purse strap and stared at the glowing display of numbers as they descended eleven floors. Mr. Chen scratched his forehead with the tip of his pinkie. He was hoping she wouldn't care about the subway station.

The elevator doors slid open, and Mr. Chen gestured for the woman to go ahead. They walked through the lobby, past the double glass doors that led into the garden. As had happened before, Mr. Chen experienced the curious sensation of leaving behind some part of himself. Everything suddenly was light and color and air. So many flowers he didn't know the names of, the same color as autumn leaves, gold and burgundy and rust. Sunlight streamed through the glass vault of the ceiling, yet because the conservatory was air-conditioned it was cooler here than inside the apartment.

"Beautiful garden," Marnie Wilson said, staring at the chrysanthemums.

"Yes, beautiful," Mr. Chen agreed.

They stood in silence for a minute longer, and then Mr. Chen awkwardly cleared his throat. The moment had come to ask whether she was interested in the apartment, but before he could speak, he saw her pale lips moving slowly. " 'And their soul shall be as a watered garden,' " she murmured, " 'and they shall not sorrow any more at all.' "

Mr. Chen flushed but did not say anything.

She turned toward him, gently patting her skirt, which clung to the flowers. "I would like to live here," she said.

Mr. Chen showed his wife the security deposit check for eight hundred dollars. They had signed the lease that very afternoon, and the Christian lady would advance the first month's rent by the end of the week. Mrs. Chen was happy, but she pretended to find fault with her husband. "You were too hasty," she said. "Why didn't you check her references?"

"She looked respectable," Mr. Chen said. "She works at a travel agency near the apartment."

"And how did she dress?"

"A suit. Like she was educated."

Mrs. Chen snorted. "Christians are crazy, smiling at you all the time. Your child dies, and they say you should be happy."

Mr. Chen sighed, looking out the front window. "She didn't seem like that." From the living room, he could see one of the two cypresses that grew beside their front door. Twelve years ago, when they first moved into their house, the trees had barely reached Mr. Chen's hip, but over the years they had grown into dark, thin spires. When their son was diagnosed with cancer, Mrs. Chen wanted her husband to cut them down. "They're bad luck," she said. "They overshadow our house."

Mr. Chen grew angry at his wife's suggestion. "Don't be silly. Chopping down two trees won't make his sickness go away."

The tumor steadily advanced until the doctors told the Chens that their son's only chance at recovery was surgery. The Chens relented because by this time they were hoping for a miracle. But how stupid they had been, Mrs. Chen wept to her husband. A person cannot live when his head is sliced open like a watermelon, Western medicine or not. Why had they let the doctors touch him? He had died on the operating table with no one to comfort him. A terrible death that no one deserves, and he was only fifteen years old.

Mrs. Chen's tongue grew more venomous after their son died. When she opened her mouth, it was as if she were spitting out words to rid herself of life's bitter taste.

In contrast, Mr. Chen became softer, less defined. He rarely talked now, and the wrinkles on his face deepened so that Mrs. Chen said his forehead resembled a tic-tac-toe board. Mrs. Chen made her words sharp to wake him up. She didn't like to see him wading through the motions of life.

Neither of them mentioned the cypresses, which continued to twist toward the sky. It was as if their mutual silence were a tacit agreement to let them grow, each willing the bad winds to keep blowing.

In October, Mr. Chen received a four-hundred-dollar check from Marnie Wilson, accompanied by a note of apology. "Not two months and already she can't pay," he muttered, showing the check to his wife. When he called her number, he heard the same toneless voice recorded on her answering machine. *And God shall wipe away all tears . . .* Mr. Chen did not wait for the message to end before he hung up the phone.

A week went by with no additional check in the mail. On Saturday afternoon, Mr. Chen decided to let his wife manage the store without him and he drove to Garden City Apartments. It usually took him forty-five minutes to drive into the city, and he had come to regard all the driving back and forth as a waste of gas and time. The worst was when people made appointments to see the apartment but then didn't show up. He would wait in the lobby, looking up from his newspaper at each person who came through the revolving doors. When an hour passed, Mr. Chen was forced to fold up his paper and drive back home. It was on such days that he believed people had no respect for each other.

In the lobby, Mr. Chen asked the doorman whether he knew if Marnie Wilson was in. "If you'll just wait a second," the doorman said, "I'll call up and see if she's there."

"No, no, I go up," Mr. Chen said. "She go out every morning?"

The doorman shook his head. "Not that I know of."

Mr. Chen took the elevator to the twelfth floor and walked down the close, dimly lit hallway. The walls were painted the color of dark moss, and the carpet was confusing for him to look at with its intertwining flowers. He knocked on the apartment door. "Miss Wilson?" He wondered if she was going to pretend not to be in.

A door opened loudly across the hallway. A large woman in a robe and sneakers peered at him from her doorway. Mr. Chen could hear her breathing through her mouth. He smiled and nodded, and the woman closed her door without saying anything.

"Miss Wilson?" he said, more softly this time. He put his ear against the door and tried to turn the knob. He hesitated before taking the key out of his pocket. If she was there, he would apologize, say that he remembered a previous tenant complaining about a leak.

"Hello," he called as he opened the door.

It was late afternoon, and a dusty gold light filtered through the windows. Mr. Chen could tell from the hushed stillness that no one was inside. He was surprised by the apartment's emptiness. Two chairs, a card table with rusting legs, a small bookcase with slanting paperbacks. A clock on the wall had stopped at 6:35. For a moment, Mr. Chen panicked, thinking the Christian lady had left her most worthless possessions behind. But then he noticed a small blue silk rug that changed to a silvery green when he walked to the other side of the room. It was the only valuable-looking thing in the apartment and at odds with the rest of her furniture.

Through the window, Mr. Chen could see the parking lot, a few trees, and the eight-lane highway. From twelve stories above, behind sealed windows, the cars glided soundlessly past.

In the bedroom, Mr. Chen was startled by the mirrors that the Christian lady had hung along the wall, at least a dozen of them, some as small as the palm of his hand. Oval and rectangular mirrors, mirrors in the shapes of triangles and suns, mirrors with smooth silver faces and dark blemishes reflecting hardly anything at all. They flickered to life whenever he moved. There was a single mattress with a wool blanket on the floor. An upturned box that she had decorated with an embroidered handkerchief and used as a night table for her Bible, lamp, and radio. He pushed open her closet door, saw her few clothes drooping from their hangers. The shelf above the rack was empty except for an old maroon hat with a wilted black feather. When he took it off the shelf, the hat was stiff and light in his hands, the velvet marred by dark, oily spots.

On his way out, Mr. Chen saw two sun-faded photographs on the refrigerator door. Two little girls in orange bikinis were standing in a plastic pool in the front yard of a house. One girl's mouth was open in a scream of delight, her hands clutching her hair, her child's belly exposed to the camera, as the older girl gazed quietly on. In the second photograph, the same two girls were dressed in bright-striped shirts and bell-bottoms and together held a large squash in their arms. The younger one squinted in the sun, her lips parted, showing two large front teeth. Mr. Chen thought the older one, the girl who seemed more distant and self-possessed, was Marnie Wilson.

He let himself out of the apartment, quietly shutting the door behind him.

He found the Christian lady downstairs in the garden. She sat on a bench beside the roses, her head bowed over a book, her lips moving silently over the words. She wore a plaid gray dress and short black-laced boots. There was a painstaking neatness in her appearance, which for some reason made Mr. Chen feel sorry for her. Her smooth brown hair was pulled back too tightly, revealing a high, pale forehead. She looked up at him, and Mr. Chen began to smile, but she hastily glanced down at her book, her index finger moving rapidly across the page.

"Miss Wilson?"

Her shoulder blades stiffened, and she stared at her book a moment longer before raising her head. Mr. Chen pretended to look around the garden. "You like this place," he said.

She shut her book, her fingers still caught between the pages.

"I receive your letter. You say you have a job?"

She gave a slight cough, clearing her throat. "It was only temporary."

Mr. Chen nodded. "You find another job." She set her book down on the bench without saying anything. "Why don't you ask help from parents? Your parents can help, right?"

She looked down at her lap, studying her hands as if they didn't belong to her. Then, in a calm voice, she told Mr. Chen that her parents were dead. With one hand, she smoothed the creases in her dress.

Mr. Chen was silent. He felt a curious lightness take over his body, as if he were watching proceedings from far away. For the first time, he wondered if the Christian lady was a liar. "Oh, too bad," he finally said. He was too embarrassed to bring up the subject of money now.

She looked at him, smiling faintly. "I will give you the money as soon as I can."

"Okay," Mr. Chen mumbled, turning away. "Thank you."

On the way home, Mr. Chen found himself stuck in traffic, amid a procession of alien, glittering cars. The image of the Christian lady sitting in the garden with her eyes half-closed and her lips moving seemed unreal to him, a fragment of a dream. A car honked, and Mr. Chen realized that the cars ahead of his had begun to move. He pushed the gas too hard, and the engine roared to life as his car leapt forward.

When he came home, he found his wife on the bed propped up against her pillows. She was wearing cotton pajamas, the seat of her pants marred by faint circles of blood. She had scrubbed them again and again until they were only terra-cotta outlines. "Do you know what day this is?" she asked him.

Mr. Chen looked at her blankly.

"Today is our anniversary," she said. She narrowed her eyes, looking at him carefully. "I'm not surprised that you should forget. There isn't anything happy to remember about this day. Do you remember we spent two hundred dollars for the reception? Ha! That was a lot of money to us then."

"It still is a lot of money," he said.

"You always were stingy in your heart," she said. "That woman can't pay a few hundred dollars, and you go sniffing for it like a dog."

"What do you want?" Mr. Chen muttered. "You complain if I go, and you complain if I don't."

"That's because you make me sick," she said. "Do you hear that? Nothing you do will make me happy." She began to cry and wiped her tears away with the back of her hand. She got off the bed and went into the bathroom, slamming the door. Mr. Chen heard a sound of something smashing. He was silent for a moment. "Mingli," he said. He knocked on the door. He could hear his wife sobbing. "Open the door."

"Go away," she cried.

Mr. Chen went back to their bedroom. He sat down on the edge of their bed in a stupor. In a few minutes, he heard her opening the door. "Do you know what I regret the most?" she said. Her face was a terrible sight. He could stand any viciousness from his wife, but he couldn't stand her tears. They made him deeply afraid.

"I don't want to hear," he said.

"Do you remember that time when he cried outside our door? He was four years old and he cried outside our door wanting to sleep with us. We didn't let him in because we didn't want to spoil him. He cried for an hour maybe, and we listened to him for all that time, and when he was quiet, we thought he had gone back to bed. But in the morning, we found him lying outside our door, his forehead burning with fever. Do you remember?"

"Yes," Mr. Chen said.

Mrs. Chen got into bed, turning her back away from him. "That memory makes me feel bad," she said. "I can't ever forget it. It's what I regret the most." She reached over and turned off her light.

Mr. Chen received a call from the apartment management. People in the building were beginning to wonder about the woman who sat all day in the conservatory. "They thought at first she didn't live here, that she came off the streets," the office manager told Mr. Chen. "A resident saw her distributing pamphlets under people's doors." The manager laughed uncomfortably.

Mr. Chen grunted.

"Believe me, we don't have anything against your tenant. But I thought you should know about her behavior. Maybe you could talk to her?"

"Me? What can I do? She hasn't paid rent for two months." The week before, the Christian lady had sent Mr. Chen a check for three hundred dollars along with a handwritten note. *Once I win my case with the government, I will be able to pay you the money I owe.*

"Is that so?" The manager sounded pleasantly surprised, then immediately lowered his voice. "You are the landlord, after all."

Mr. Chen sighed as he hung up the phone. He dug around

in the closet for his typewriter, which he used for official business only, and poking at the keys with two fingers he fashioned a reply to the Christian lady. *I hear no more excuses. I come on Monday to speak to you.*

On Monday evening, he drove to Garden City Apartments, wondering whether she would be in. The weatherman had predicted a storm, and the air had turned breezy and cold. Mr. Chen gripped the steering wheel whenever he felt the wind nudging his car into the other lane. The sky was dark and clear, without a hint of rain.

In the apartment building, he was surprised to find the Christian lady's door half-open. He glimpsed through the crack and saw her kneeling on the floor. At first, he thought she was patting an animal, but then he saw that she was straightening the fringe of her rug. He knocked on the door, and she told him to come in. She stood up, slowly wiping her hands against her skirt. She wore a blouse with tiny red flowers embroidered around the collar.

"Hello," Mr. Chen said, nodding. He continued to stand even though she motioned to one of the chairs. "I like to talk to you about this check."

"You must forgive me," she said. "It's all I have."

Mr. Chen flushed. "I can't afford to have tenant that cannot pay," he said. "Isn't there someone—sister maybe—who can help?" Marnie Wilson gazed back at him without any expression in her eyes. "You go to church, right? Someone from your church can help you?"

She looked as if she were about to speak, but then she closed her mouth. She gave her head a barely perceptible shake.

"Maybe you find a roommate," Mr. Chen persisted. "Someone to move in here, someone you can talk to, you pay only half the rent?"

"I like living here alone."

"What about work? You work, right?" She was silent, and Mr. Chen closed his eyes, shaking his head. A sound of hissing escaped from his teeth. "I'm sorry. You find another place to live."

The Christian lady turned her head to look out the window. "I don't like to go outside."

Mr. Chen looked at her. "Bad weather," he murmured.

From the windowsill, she picked up a green and silver box that looked as if it were meant to hold cigars. She traced the pattern with a finger before passing it to him. Mr. Chen held the box awkwardly in his hands. It was decorated with intersecting green and black lines in the shape of diamonds and three-petaled flowers with a streak of red in the center. He fumbled with the lid, thinking there might be something inside, but the box was empty. He saw only his blurred face upside down in the warped metal.

The Christian lady said he could keep it, but Mr. Chen shook his head, looking for a place to set it down. She said he could give it back once she paid him the money she owed. Mr. Chen stood with the box in his hands, feeling suddenly depressed. "You never go out?"

She pointed to the window. Mr. Chen could see the first drops of rain tapping the pane. He looked down to the parking lot and could hardly make out his small green car in the dusk, everything coated in a pale silver sheen. The trees were stirring to life, dry leaves circling the asphalt. It was a quiet world, Mr. Chen thought, waiting to be seized.

"It makes me afraid," she said. "I think terrible things will happen."

He heard the wind rising, an ocean in his ears. He could see lights flickering in the distance. The woman stood gazing out the window with her back toward him. His own body felt vacant and cold. The apartment had become a still life, he and the woman faceless, incorporated into the silence of the room.

The woman turned, and Mr. Chen took a step back. Though her mouth was moving, he couldn't hear anything. Only the sound of his blood in his ears.

"Mr. Chen, are you well? Would you like some tea?"

He shook his head. His body had broken out into a cold sweat, and he realized he was shivering. "Sorry," he whispered hoarsely.

"Mr. Chen, why don't you sit down and rest?"

"No, I'm okay," he muttered, moving toward the door.

"I promise to pay you soon."

Mr. Chen barely nodded as he shut the door behind him.

Driving home through the rain, he caught glimpses of branches and debris scattered on the road. Black leaves streamed in the wind, slapping his windshield, getting tangled in the wipers. Mr. Chen felt as if his mind had been infected. At home, he found his wife sitting at the kitchen table drinking tea. When she saw him, she raised her eyebrows. "Well?"

"Nothing," he muttered.

"You need to kick her out."

Mr. Chen took off his coat and hung it in the closet. He had not known what to do with the box and had hidden it underneath the seat of his car.

"She can't continue living there for free," Mrs. Chen said.

"She isn't well," he told her. "Something wrong with her head."

That night, he dreamed that he'd gone to the apartment again, but it had turned into an endless cavern of rooms. An orange cat followed at his heels, and this made him worry that the management would charge him a fine. When he found the

Christian lady, she was standing before a mirror, wearing purple eye shadow and drinking a glass of wine. "My mother," she said, gesturing to the wall. Mr. Chen realized that what he'd thought was a mirror was actually a photograph of a woman sitting morosely in a chair, her thin, dark hair plastered to her skull, her eyes vacant and heavily lidded. A white bow in the shape of a rose was pinned to the front of her long black dress. Her lips seemed to be waxed shut, and she grasped a startled baby in her lap between both hands. The Christian lady laughed. "No need to feel sorry for her," she told him.

Mr. Chen wondered about his dream. He knew so little about the Christian lady. When he imagined her, he always saw her alone, reading or looking out a window, gazing into one of her mirrors or studying her meaningless collection of boxes.

December arrived, and he did not hear from her. No checks or apologies. He tried calling her number, but there was a recorded message saying the line had been disconnected.

"That woman is robbing us blind," Mrs. Chen said. "But you continue to act as if we are running a charity organization."

Mr. Chen felt a terrible pressure in his head. "What can I do?" he burst out. "Throw her onto the street?"

"Don't be naïve," his wife said.

He drove to Garden City Apartments the next day. No one answered the door, and he let himself in. The card table, the chairs, the bookcase—all her things were in the places he remembered, untouched, as in a museum display. The silent, airless room made him feel trapped. It was difficult to imagine how anyone could live here.

In the kitchen, the photograph of the two little girls standing in the plastic pool was slipping from its magnet. Mr. Chen straightened the photograph and opened the refrigerator door. There was a box of cereal, a shrunken apple, and a jar of floating olives. They seemed like odd artifacts in the empty white space of the refrigerator.

In the bedroom, the Christian lady's mirrors glimmered faintly as Mr. Chen walked by. The mattress had been stripped of its sheets, and dust had gathered in balls in the corners of the room.

He heard a sound of shifting from the closet.

"Miss Wilson?" he said aloud.

He tried to slide the closet door back, but it got stuck along its groove. The sleeves of her dresses poked through. In the dark of the closet, he discerned something moving, a tangled mass of hair, though he wasn't sure if it was a face or the back of a head. He looked down and saw chapped heels protruding from a blanket. The Christian lady lay on her stomach, her nightgown tightly wound around her body, her hands hidden beneath her. Her body was stiff, yet she seemed to be struggling underwater. She turned her head to look at him, and her eyes had a shiny faraway luster, as if she were drugged. Mr. Chen thought she looked like some kind of animal. He did not say anything but hastily slid the closet door shut and left the apartment.

At the grocery store, his wife sat on a stool in front of the cash register watching Chinese videos. "So are you going to kick her out?" she said.

"I will call the lawyer that the Zhangs used," he replied.

His wife continued to watch her video, but after a while her lips twisted into a strange smile. "That poor woman," she said.

•   •   •

Mr. Chen could not sleep. Though it was winter, he didn't need a blanket because his wife's body burned like a furnace all year long. When they were newlyweds, he had joked with her about the temperature of her body, pretending to scorch his fingers whenever he touched her skin. She was a young woman then; her passion had been a great deal of her charm. But her temper had increased with age, and Mr. Chen feared that his wife was like a piece of burning wood that appears firm and unyielding until it suddenly collapses.

He turned over in bed and looked at the red eyes of the clock. Three a.m. In four hours, both he and his wife would be up—she to open their store, he to drive to Garden City Apartments. He wondered if the Christian lady would be gone by that time, the apartment as clean and empty as it had been five months ago, not a sign that she had ever lived there.

She had never shown up for the hearing. Mr. Chen learned about her absence from his lawyer. The judge had set a month's deadline for her to pay what rent she owed, but she hadn't been able to do this. Instead, she sent Mr. Chen a Christmas card. On the front, a quiet, even desolate painting of a lake turned blue with ice, a few spruce trees buried in a drift of snow. In mournful, slanting letters, she wished him a merry Christmas with a promise to pay back the money she owed. He turned over in bed once more, flipping his pillow to get to its cool side.

His sleep was no longer good. Even before his son became ill, Mr. Chen often woke up in the middle of the night, his temples smarting as his thoughts turned inexorably against him. He would escape by going to the bathroom, flicking on the light, and then he would wander down the hallway to check on his son. He would stop by the doorway, listening to his son's breathing, heavy and asthmatic in the darkness. Usually he had kicked his blanket to the ground. Mr. Chen would stoop to pick it up, awkwardly pulling at the corners of the blanket to cover him.

It was Mr. Chen's lasting regret that they had never been close. His son had preferred his mother's company. Somehow Mr. Chen had never been able to find the right words. His questions were always gruff, and he didn't know how to smooth out his tongue. Where were you? Did you eat? Why didn't you wear your jacket? Have you finished your homework? To these questions, his son had replied in monosyllables. What Mr. Chen meant to ask was whether he was hungry, whether he was cold, whether there was anything that he lacked which Mr. Chen could offer? He hadn't been able to show his love in any other way than by providing for him, and so he gave him food to eat, clothes to wear, and a bed to sleep in. These things hadn't been enough to keep him alive.

Mr. Chen's head felt swollen as he waited for the sky to lighten. At seven a.m., he rose from bed, his brain throbbing with a swarm of useless images. His wife's face was slack against her pillow, her dry lips parted slightly. She seemed to be lost in sleep as he stood watching her, but then her eyes opened. "I'm leaving soon," he said. Mrs. Chen stared vacantly at him, and he wondered if she had understood what he said. "I'll be back before noon," he told her. She lay there, stiff and unblinking, and Mr. Chen turned away to change.

When he returned to the bedroom, the bed was empty and his wife was no longer in sight.

He found her in the garage, sitting in the passenger seat of his car. She wore a brown sweater with large yellow flowers and brown wool pants, and she was getting her makeup out of her purse when he opened the door. "That woman is a rat," she said. "I'd like nothing more than to sweep her out with a broom."

"What about the store?" he asked.

She smeared powder along her forehead. "I put up a sign yesterday."

When they got onto the beltway, there were rows of gleaming cars stretched into the distance ahead of them. They sat and waited, the inside of the car filling up with exhaust. By the time they reached Garden City Apartments, they were half an hour late. Large wreaths decorated with white and gold ribbons hung in the entranceway, even though Christmas had passed almost a month ago. The lobby was crowded, and when Mr. Chen inhaled the scent of a woman's perfume, he experienced the same light-headed sickness he felt in department stores. Cold air blew along the back of his neck as people passed in and out of the revolving doors. Boxes were already stacked along the wall, and the movers he had hired were busy unloading furniture from the freight elevator. A man in a gray suit came up to him. "George Chen?" he inquired.

Mr. Chen nodded.

The man shook his hand and said he was from the justice court.

"Sorry to be so late," Mr. Chen muttered.

"Nothing to worry about. Your apartment is almost all cleared out. Miss Wilson will be coming down shortly."

"I want to go up and see," his wife told him in Chinese. Before Mr. Chen could say anything, she stepped onto the next elevator, the doors closing quickly behind her.

"An odd woman," the man from the justice court remarked. Mr. Chen thought at first that the man was referring to his wife. But then the elevator doors opened, and Marnie Wilson appeared, a faint smile on her lips. Her dark hair was pulled back into a tiny bun, and she wore the same blue suit that she had worn on the day that Mr. Chen had first shown her the apartment. He wondered what she had placed inside the small black suitcase that she clutched at her side. She stepped off the elevator, followed by two policemen. The doorman immediately approached her. "Miss Wilson," he said, looking embarrassed. "I'm sorry, but you can't leave your furniture and boxes here."

The Christian lady's face tightened, red splotches appearing on her skin. "Please," she said.

"I'm sorry, Miss Wilson, I truly am, but our manager has informed me that you can't leave your things in the lobby."

The movers were already beginning to carry her boxes and furniture outside to the street. Mr. Chen watched as the Christian lady dragged her suitcase across the lobby through the revolving doors. She stood nervously on the sidewalk beside her possessions, and people stared at her and at her things as they walked by. The movers continued to dump boxes and furniture on the ground, her possessions growing and spreading into an island around her feet. Everything was in a pile, jumbled together. Her chairs, her table, her bookcase, her rug, her mattress. The movers departed, and she was left standing alone amid the heap. She picked up her suitcase, walked a few steps, then set it back down again.

Mr. Chen tapped her on the shoulder, and she flew around to look at him. "I'm sorry about all this," he said. She stared at him with dazed eyes, and Mr. Chen looked away, pretending to study her possessions. "What are you going to do? You have so many things." He regretted his words as soon as they were spoken. The Christian lady owned very little actually. It had taken the movers only a half hour to clear out the apartment.

"I'm sorry," he repeated, shaking his head. "I hoped you already moved."

The Christian lady's mouth trembled as she smiled. "I was

so happy to live here," she said. She fumbled in her pocket and pressed something cold and silver into his palm. Mr. Chen saw that he was holding the key to the apartment.

In the lobby, there was no sign of his wife. The elevator was open, as if waiting for him, and Mr. Chen rode up twelve floors in silence. In the dim hallway, he hesitated for a moment, trying to remember which way to turn. On the door, the Christian lady had taped a note in neat handwriting. *Forgive, and ye shall be forgiven,* it read.

He found his wife inside the empty apartment. She stood in front of a window, her arms folded across her chest as she looked down at the city. The room was perfectly bare, just as he had imagined, but he knew he wouldn't be able to forget that the Christian lady had lived here.

"Do you remember when we first saw this apartment?" his wife said. "We thought everything was going to be better then."

"Mingli," he said, and his voice sounded strange to him. It did not sound like his own. He wanted to say something, to ask her pardon, but he could only touch her sleeve as she continued to stare out the window.

"I feel . . ." she said, and she covered her eyes with one hand. "I feel it would be easy to live in an apartment like this. I could live here for the rest of my life."

Mr. Chen laid his hand on the back of her head. He could feel her scalp's warmth through the dry threads of her hair. Outside, there was winter, gray buildings against a white sky. From where he stood, he saw tiny cars inching along the highway through a world that had fallen into silence.

ACKNOWLEDGMENTS

For their generous support during the writing of this book, I would like to thank the Fine Arts Work Center in Provincetown, the Wisconsin Institute for Creative Writing, Colgate University, the MacDowell Colony, and the Rona Jaffe Foundation.

So many people have helped me with these stories. There are others, too, whose friendship and conversation were invaluable to me as I wrote this book. I wish to thank them all for their contribution to this work.

I am grateful as well to my teachers Kevin Canty, Debra Earling, Deirdre McNamer, and Joy Williams and to my fellow graduate students at the University of Montana. Special heartfelt thanks to Helen Atsma, Esi Edugyan, Wendy Erman, Matt Freidson, Tamara Guirado, Nancy Hwang, Jayne Yaffe Kemp, Linda Mao, Sheila McGuinness, Michael Mezzo, Shimon Tanaka, and Amy Williams.

ABOUT THE AUTHOR

Frances Hwang is a graduate of Brown University and the University of Montana. She has held fellowships at the Fine Arts Work Center in Provincetown, the Wisconsin Institute for Creative Writing, and Colgate University. A past recipient of the Rona Jaffe Foundation Writer's Award, she lives in Berkeley, California.

Reading Group Guide

Transparency

Stories by

FRANCES HWANG

A conversation with Frances Hwang

You have studied writing at Brown University and the University of Montana. Before attending Brown, did you know you wanted to be a writer? How has formally studying the craft of writing been beneficial to you?

I was in the eleventh grade when I thought that maybe I could be a writer. Until then, it seemed outside the scope of possibility, even though writing was something I was always interested in. What changed for me was simply having a close friend who also wrote and who was even more impractical and idealistic than I was. Somehow it no longer seemed like such a crazy thing to want to devote my life to writing. If the world thought I was foolish, it was comforting to know there was someone else who shared my delusions.

Finding a community of writers might be one of the best reasons to go to graduate school to study creative writing. As a writer, you face rejection at every turn, and what's worse, people often regard you as naïve, lazy, and unfortunate. So one of the things that makes this a little more bearable is finding others, like you, who are struggling to put words down on the page and who don't question the validity of what you're doing. It certainly can turn the solitary endeavor of writing into a more hopeful, less lonely one.

Before going to the University of Montana, I must say, I was drifting as a writer. I had no sense of audience (that is, when I wrote, I didn't have any consideration for my reader), I wasn't reading contemporary fiction, and I didn't have friends who were serious, practicing writers. In short, I was writing in a vacuum, and the result was incredibly stilted, pretentious stuff. I had a grandiose desire to write brilliantly, to write sentences of *genius,* but this ended up paralyzing me. Going to school for creative writing was a nice dose of reality and allowed me to come down from the ether. I had to start from the very beginning, with no pretensions and no ego, just a desire to communicate as truthfully as I could.

Some of the stories in Transparency *involve people who have limited interaction with society. Your character Marnie Wilson, for instance, stays in her apartment and seems unwilling or afraid to go out. Why do you think you're interested in writing about this subject?*

It definitely wasn't a conscious obsession, but I do notice that it's a recurring theme in my work. Maybe it has to do with my profession, how I have to shut myself up in a room and not socialize if I want to focus and write. It also seems to me that modern life can be very isolating. The world is smaller and in a sense more connected through the power of the media, but we ourselves seem to be diminished, made numb, by the constant barrage of information and entertainment we view when we turn on our televisions and computers. We might not know our neighbors, but we do know the latest celebrity gossip. So when I write about shut-ins, I'm trying to touch upon this feeling of disconnection and unreality that pervades our lives amid all the confusion and chatter.

Several years ago, when I was living in Philadelphia, an acquaintance of mine was talking about some artist or thinker who believed that as humans we're fated to live apart from one another, trapped inside our own separate rooms. There are windows we can look out of, and this is how we communicate, but ultimately we're separated by glass. This person I knew said that he might have to find a key or break a window, but whatever it took, he would do all that he could to get out of that room. I was struck by what he said. All of us have a hope for connection, a deep longing to get out of our separate selves.

In "Blue Hour," Iris likes the idea that people are always remarking on her resemblance to Laura, mistaking the two friends for sisters. But Laura tells Iris that they don't look alike at all and that "people are always confusing one Asian for another." No other mention is made of the ethnicity of these two characters. Was this a conscious choice of yours?

As I wrote that story, Iris and Laura's ethnicity wasn't a crucial detail for me. They could have been any ethnicity, and the point of "Blue Hour" would still be the same. Iris is worried about her fading friendship with Laura and her imperfect, rather tenuous relationship with Paul, but she isn't obsessing about her Asian identity. And yet I deliberately included Laura's observation because I've found that unless a character is specifically labeled as such or given an ethnic-sounding name, readers will probably assume the character is white. I wanted to make it clear to the reader that Iris and Laura are Asian, maybe for the perverse reason that the story has little or nothing to do with being Asian. I think some readers tend to assume that an Asian character's experience is primarily shaped by and concerned with being Asian. But you can't reduce a person's experience to his or her ethnicity. Similarly, there's often an assumption that a minority writer's subject matter is going to be dealing heavily with race and culture. I'm afraid it's a way of pigeonholing and even dismissing that writer's work. There's no doubt that my ethnicity informs my identity and my writing, but it's not the only subject I want to write about.

How has your reading life informed your writing life? Which writers have most influenced your work?

I have strong, vivid memories of the books I read as a child and the joy I felt while reading them. There was nothing as wonderful as leaving behind dull reality and falling into another world—and all I had to do was open up a book. More than anything, it was this love of reading that made me want to write.

The writers I feel most strongly about are the Russians. Tolstoy, Dostoevsky, and Chekhov are my holy triumvirate. They seem to go the furthest in terms of everything—the heart, the mind, the spirit. Everything. Other writers who have left an indelible impression on me are Joyce, Woolf, Faulkner, and Proust, just to name a few. Probably the writers whose influence I was most conscious of as I wrote this collection were Chekhov and Alice Munro. What I admire about Chekhov is how clearly he sees his characters, revealing their limitations in precise, devastating ways, yet never losing compassion for them. And Munro is doing something so delightful and unexpected with the short story. I've found that I can't ever predict where her stories will go and how they will end. She manages to surprise me every time, yet I never feel tricked by her because somehow her surprises are those that life affords us.

What I love about fiction is how it encourages us to step outside the boundaries of our lives and to empathize with people whom we'd never otherwise meet. This ability to identify with others, to understand their situations and be moved by their experiences, is probably the most important thing fiction does for us. In this way, I believe reading literature humanizes us.

Questions and topics for discussion

1. Agnes loathes her father's new wife, Lily, in the story "The Old Gentleman." Did you feel any sympathy for Lily? Why or why not?

2. In "A Visit to the Suns," June is asked to encourage her cousin Helen to leave the oppressive religious group that Helen recently joined. In the end, though, June doesn't push Helen to change her ways. Should she have?

3. The characters in "The Modern Age" sit around a table telling one another "persecuted ancestor stories." Are there any similar stories in your family's history? If not, what other types of family stories have been passed down to you?

4. In "Intruders," Susan discovers a note from Andrea written in her diary and tears the page out because she says she doesn't want Andrea's thoughts to be mistaken for her own. Do you think Susan resembles Andrea in any way? How are they different from each other?

5. In "Garden City," Mr. Chen ultimately evicts his tenant, Marnie Wilson, from her apartment. Should he have

acted differently? How would you have responded in his situation?

6. Do you see any parallels in plot or character in "Transparency" and "Garden City"? What cultural and familial misunderstandings arise in both stories?

7. The protagonist in "The Modern Age" says at the end of the story, "As for my boyfriend and me, we had been together for over a year, yet not once had the word *love* been spoken between us. Our hearts seemed too small for such a word to pass between our lips." What was your reaction to this statement? Do the relationships described in Hwang's collection seem familiar to you? Why?

8. "Sonata for the Left Hand" is composed of three sections, each part taking place in a different city and among different characters in the narrator's life. What did Hwang accomplish by writing this story in the way she did? Did the three parts of the story come together for you by the end?

9. What do the stories in *Transparency* say about solitude? Is it a cross to bear, a choice that encourages personal strength and freedom, or a bit of both? Is solitude something you seek in your own life, or do you try to avoid it?